LITERARY OUTLAW

A PULP FICTION MAGAZINE | ISSUE #7

IN THIS ISSUE:

LITERARY OUTLAW #7
Copyright © 2024 by LiteraryOutlawLLC

www.literaryoutlaw.com

NOW COMES THE BRINGER OF BLIGHT

BY ED GOSNEY

Day 1

Maybe I should call it day 15, which is closer to the truth, but 15 has never been a good number for me. Besides, I didn't have this garage-sale laptop until this morning, which means Day 1 is appropriate. So this is how I'm starting it. And if I'm the one writing it down, telling the truth of what's going on, then who's to say I'm wrong?

This is kinda weird, I guess, but I've always liked to write. Never had much to say before, but if I were a reporter, this would probably win a Pulitzer. Or something. If we had Internet maybe I'd post it to a blog . . . eventually. After it's over, I guess it would be safe.

So it's been 15 days since I found out that Zach Hochberg has superpowers. How long has he had them? Your guess is as good as mine. When something this big happens, most people would tell their best friend. If you're reading this, maybe you're scratching your head now. Especially if you know Zach and me. We used to do everything together, for as long as I can remember. I guess, though, that when you find yourself basically invulnerable and able to fly, and you become the most selfish person I can think of (worse than Lex Luthor!), then you *don't* tell your former best buddy. Because I was always Batman to his Superman. We've actually had conversations about what we'd do if we got superpowers, and we were like, "Dude, we'd be Power Man and Iron Fist." Super friends through and through. I guess it doesn't work that way when just one of us evolves into the most powerful teen on earth.

Back to 15 for a minute. That's how old I was when my father walked away from us. Us being me and mom. I want it written here, for the record, in case I do post this and he reads it. Nice technique at fathering, wouldn't you say? It's been close to two years now. I'm 17 and still riding a bike, because we can't afford a car. He drove away in the only one we owned. Mom rides the bus for both of her jobs. Cleaning houses in the morning and scrubbing office building toilets at night. Great legacy, dad.

We never had much money when you were here, but at least we had a car. And snail-slitheringly slow Internet service, but we had it. Not anymore. Mom sold the computer. She told me to go to the library if I need one for school assignments. Do I need to tell you how much that sucks?

Yet not everything is a negative. Today is Saturday, and I rode my bike around for a while, thinking about Zach and how to fix the problem, and that's when I saw it. A beat-up old HP laptop at a garage sale. I pulled two dollars out of my jeans and handed it over as fast as I could. The lady seemed a little embarrassed when she took a look at me (Come on, ripped jeans used to be a thing, right? And who has the time to buy new sneakers these days? They're falling apart, but they get me where I'm going.), so she said she was just about to mark it down to half price and gave me back a dollar. I took it. I mean, I'm not proud. Why should I be?

The laptop works good enough for me to write this blog. Who cares that it's ancient. Anyway, Zach will be heading out soon, and I'm going to try to track his moves. Tomorrow I'll have time to write more while mom is at church. I can report the latest on my "frenemy" and maybe fill in some of what's happened over the last couple weeks. If I live.

This is Coby Cook, signing out.

Day 2

STILL ALIVE.

It's good to have someone like you who cares, who actually listens.

OK, so I know I'm not really talking to anyone, but maybe someday, someone will be reading this. And it makes me feel a little better to pretend I'm talking this over with a friend. Because I lost my best friend. I'm just hoping now that Zach doesn't kill me first. I thought he was going to, last night. Remember when I said I was going to follow him? I did. At least for a while. Then it was him following me.

I biked over to the park across the street from the Hochberg house. Like I said, he lives in the next block, and his stupid sisters are always out front jumping rope and stuff, so I went the long way around to the back entrance of the park, just past the swings. Some big hedges are facing the street, so I laid down my bike and hid there. Man, was it boring. Zach has three sisters. The oldest, Lydia, is 15, Katie is 12, and Alisa is 11 now. They were sitting on the porch, yakking away nonstop about boys for about three hours it seemed, and my legs started

cramping up as much as my brain from the stupid talk. Finally, their mom yelled out the front window to come in and start getting ready for bed. I can't tell you how long it was until Zach came outside because I'd fallen asleep. The screen door of their house makes a loud creaking noise, which brought me awake. I wiped some drool off the corner of my mouth, watched the direction he headed, then crawled out of the hedges and hopped on my bike.

Zach turned the corner at the end of his block. Going downtown, I figured. Better businesses to knock off compared to this neighborhood. Anyway, he can fly, and pretty fast, too, so I quickly pedaled in pursuit, and when I rounded the corner I crashed right into him. He'd jumped out from behind a van and when my front tire made contact, both my bike and I went flying in opposite directions.

Before he gave me the chance to lick my wounds, he picked me up with one hand and set me on my feet.

"You need to stop following me."

Just like that. No "Hi Coby, sorry we don't hang out anymore," or "Hey, sorry I forgot to tell you that I've developed superhuman strength now."

I'm not a tough guy at all, and I'll be the first to tell you I felt so groggy that I wanted to be back under the big hedge, asleep with drool on my face. When the street light above us started buzzing, I almost jumped out of my shoes. I could have folded right then, but instead I took a deep breath and got to the point.

"When were you going to tell me?" I felt sorta brave when I said it. There was attitude behind my words. But when I saw the look in his eyes, I realized I'd made a mistake. He didn't say anything, though. He just kept penetrating my brain with his eyes.

A car turned the corner and Zach broke eye contact because of the glare from the headlights, so I took the opportunity to go move my bike. Not that it would do any good as a getaway vehicle from crazy Zach, but I didn't want the car to hit it. Because I'm a good guy, unlike him.

"I don't get it," I said when I pushed my bike over to the side of the road where he was now standing. "I mean, we actually talked about what we'd do if we got powers and stuff. I thought we were like Captain America and Spider-Man, battling the forces of evil, but you're more like Darkseid."

Sometimes when you've been friends forever, you know how to strike a nerve, and at that moment I'm fairly certain that's what happened. I could be wrong, but I thought I read shame on his face. He looked down at his shoes and fidgeted a bit, and I thought I'd brought him back from the abyss.

Then he raised his head and peered into my eyes with a supervillain stare. "Yeah. We said stuff like that when we were twelve."

It felt like the temperature dropped a couple dozen degrees, and I backed up a few steps.

"You know how much money I've brought home over the last couple weeks?" I knew he didn't expect me to answer so I sat down on the curb. Whenever we have a serious conversation we sit down and talk it out.

"Listen," Zach said, getting a little fidgety. I waited for him to go on, and it seemed like forever. If he still felt uncomfortable from what I said, that was a good thing, right?

"You want a piece of the pie, or what?"

Even before it was out of his mouth, my gut told me he'd make me an offer. My mom sure could use the money.

Everyone in this neighborhood could use the money. I had to think, and when I'm under pressure, I get nervous and sometimes get a little too sarcastic. "So are you turning all Robin Hood on us now? Steal from the rich and give to the poor?"

He got ticked off and started walking away.

"Wait Zach, it's not that I don't appreciate the gesture, but you need to stop before you or somebody else gets hurt."

Walking backwards now, Zach spat on the street and shook his head. "I can't get hurt, Coby. Someone shot me a couple nights ago, but the bullet didn't penetrate. Nothing can stop me." He pulled a ski mask out of his pocket, slipped it over his head, turned around, and leaped into the air.

In seconds I was on my bike and zooming down the street as fast as I could go, trying to keep up.

"I'll tell everyone who you are," I screamed. "I'm gonna go call the police because you have to be stopped." Dogs started barking and a couple porch lights came on, and before I could blink, my bike was ten feet below me and we were soaring past the trees. I closed my eyes, figuring he'd toss me into the street, and I'd die or get paralyzed or something.

I don't know how long we flew like that, but I knew if we didn't stop soon I'd vomit, and I made sure to tell him. Then we landed and I sank to my knees, trying to pull my heart back into my chest. When I opened my eyes I couldn't see much. There was one weak lightbulb on the side of a brick building, and I could tell we were on some old concrete parking lot, with lots of cracks and spray-painted symbols all over it.

"You tell anyone, and there'll be plenty more of this," Zach said, pulling me to my feet and slapping my stomach.

Well, it looked like a slap, but he has super strength now, and it knocked the wind—and probably my spleen—right out of me. Then he started flicking his fingers on my arms and legs. I couldn't believe how painful it felt, and at the time, no kidding, I sort of wanted to die and just get it over with. "Don't forget to keep your mouth shut, or next time will be so much worse," he said, then flew away.

All in all, a pretty rotten day. Except for the fact that mom has been making a little extra money and bought a deeply discounted TV with WiFi, added Internet, and now we're no longer in the dark ages.

This is Coby Cook, signing out.

Day 3

THE WORST PART ABOUT GETTING HOME last night was figuring out where Zach left me. Besides it being so dark there, clouds covered the night sky and I couldn't even see the moon. Once I recovered enough from the beating Zach gave me, I stood up and found my way out of the parking lot and just started walking along the street. There were no cars, which was spooky enough, but no people, either. My arms broke out in gooseflesh, which actually kind of hurt because of all the finger flicks from that jerk, Hochberg.

When I got to the corner, there was a streetlight and I could read the street sign above me. Maple and 4th Avenue. Ugh. That left me about three miles from home. And every step hurt. It was pretty obvious to me that Zach meant business. Leave him alone, don't tell any-one, and I wouldn't get hurt anymore. But that's not the right thing to do, and if he knows me at all, it won't surprise him that I'm not giving up my crusade to stop him. At any cost.

How long did it take me to get home? Probably over an hour, but I didn't really know. It felt like forever, and a couple times I hid behind parked cars when I saw people. Even though it was Sunday night, and getting late, people were out roaming around. As far as I know there aren't any gangs around here, but I wasn't taking chances. And with my body feeling so sore, being a bit of a chicken seemed to be my only option. I tried playing hero earlier and look where that got me.

When I got home I popped a couple pain pills mom keeps in the medicine cabinet then grabbed a Coke and turned on the TV. I should have just gone to bed, but to be honest I felt a little scared that Zach might decide to come in and finish me off, and I didn't want to die in my sleep. If my mom had been here, maybe I would have felt differently, but she wouldn't be home for a while because she got an extra cleaning assignment at some hotel. Something about a weekend convention and needing extra hands. I needed extra hands to help me pound on Zach. But if bullets couldn't penetrate his skin, what good would punches do?

I didn't go to school today. My body is just too sore. My muscles are bruised, and my bones are aching. I told my mom I felt like I might vomit, which isn't too far from the truth.

After she left for work, I crawled back in bed and tried to get some sleep. My night was full of tossing and turning, and it didn't matter if I flipped on my right side or left side or back or stomach, it all hurt. I keep a pile of my favorite comic books on my nightstand and started read-ing an old issue of Marvel Team-Up I'd found with my dad's stuff in the base-ment. You'd think that if Spider-Man and Howard the Duck could fight on the same side, so could Zach and I. But at this point we're more like Elmer Fudd and Bugs Bunny. Only there's nothing funny about it. I didn't want to be depressed so I got up, popped more pain relief pills, grabbed a pack of Pop-Tarts and a can of Coke because it was the easiest breakfast I could think of, and binge-watched Fuller House on Netflix. Don't judge me. It was the easiest way to get Zach out of my head for a few hours.

Somewhere along the fifth or sixth episode in, my mind started drifting back to a couple weeks ago. The images on the screen were replaced with…well, you guessed it: the fateful day that the hero makes a shocking discovery that his best friend is a supervillain.

When it happened, it was kind of late, maybe close to 9:30 p.m., and since my mom was working, I biked over to Zach's so we could hang out for a while. There are five stairs leading up to the Hochberg porch, and as typical, I do a little stutter step and jump to the third step, then spring on to the porch. Zach always did it and I picked it up from him. I thought I heard a noise above me, and I was reminded how for years Zach's room faced the street, and he'd sneak out his window, walk across the little roof above the porch, and slide down one of the support beams at the corner. One day, when he was around 14 or 15, he came sliding down only to see his mother on the porch, watching him. After that, Lydia and Katie moved into that room, and now the window in Zach's room is useless because there's a straight drop onto the concrete driveway, so no more sneaking out at night.

Then I heard the noise again and realized Zach must be opening his window, so I walked over to the edge of the porch, was just about to yell up to him, and he jumped out. My breath caught in my chest and I couldn't get anything out, because right in front of my eyes my best friend has become Superman and is flying. I mean flying, like above the trees! Okay reader, so *you* already know he can

fly, but the first time I witnessed it, I nearly cried tears of joy. It took me all of two seconds to get my head in the game, jump off the porch, and try to follow on my bike. But he was fast, it was dark, and in just seconds I couldn't tell you where he went if my life depended on it. Until the next day when I saw in the newspaper that someone broke into a little convenient mart and made off with some cash. The store had security cameras, but they'd been destroyed, and the hard drive they download to turned up missing.

Did I really suspect Zach at that point? Maybe. But maybe he was playing superhero and patrolling the city at night. The crime spree didn't stop. I waited for Zach to tell me about his powers, but it was like he'd dropped off the face of the earth, at least in our friendship world. No calls, no texts, no emails. He wouldn't look at me at school. I tried to talk, and he mumbled something about not feeling well, and needed his space. He became a loner. And the stories about the mysterious robberies became a regular thing in the paper. Just small stores, nothing big like a bank. Why, I don't know. I'm sure he has his reasons.

Okay, it's getting late, my body still aches, and thinking about Zach gives me a big headache. But one last thing. Revenge is the word that keeps floating around in my head, yet this is bigger than revenge. Now it's about stopping a dangerous criminal.

This is Coby Cook, signing out.

Day 4

SOMEHOW I MADE IT THROUGH CLASSES today, but my body still hurts all over. Zach and I passed each other in the hallway a few times but he wouldn't look at me. In Mrs. Falconi's third period English class we sit right next to each other, and Hochberg did his best to make it awkward by scooting his desk away from me. And at an angle. No doubt Mrs. Falconi could tell something was up, but she's a pretty cool teacher and just let it go.

Zach had to read Hamlet's soliloquy to the class. You know, that "To be or not to be" speech, and I wondered if he thought about our situation at all. I know I did, especially the part where Hamlet says, "Thus conscience does make cowards of us all," because right now I *am* a coward. My bones and muscles ache so much, and Zach barely laid a hand on me. So my conscience is telling me to obey Hochberg and keep my mouth shut. I mean, I don't have any powers, and while I'm far from stupid, how do I outsmart someone who can easily kill me?

After school I leafed through my mom's newspaper to see what Zach did last night. A small flower shop had its cash register broken into, and the security footage is conveniently missing. The article said the mayor held a special council meeting and there will be extra police patrols around the clock. Some of the local business owners stated they'd be hiring armed guards, hoping to put a stop to this.

The whole thing is crazy. Just last month Zach and I were trading comic books and talking about some of the new video games set to launch this year. This isn't the Zach I've known my whole life, so all I can figure is that however he got these powers, it also warped his mind. And speaking of minds, I'm screwed if he has, like, mind reading powers, because the only way I'm going to get him to stop being my nemesis and robbing stores is by coming up with a plan so brilliant that he doesn't see it coming. Now I just need a plan.

This is Coby Cook, signing out.

Day 5

WHAT IN THE WORLD HAPPENED TO MY best friend? I feel like sitting here and crying instead of writing all this down, but that won't do me any good. I guess I can cry when I'm in bed tonight. All the talk at school today was about the security guard who got tossed out the window at Beltran Pharmacy. Poor guy is in a coma now and the doctors don't know if he'll make it. Word is, he lives a little outside of the city and wanted to make some extra money for his family, so he signed up to work late night shifts as part of the plan to stop the robberies. They say he has a wife and three kids. I suppose I could look up the story in the paper, but after what I heard at school, I feel sick to my stomach that Zach did this, and I don't think I want to know the extra details.

The only good that came out of today was when I bumped into Hochberg in the hall and started thinking, as strongly as I could, that he's an idiot and his stupidity would be the only part of him that wins in the end. When he didn't flinch, I tried to project (if that's the right word) my thoughts that I'd be following him tonight. Again, no response at all. So I guess he can't read my mind. Which gives me an edge, because when it comes to the two of us, I've always been smarter. And now I realize I'm also a much better person than him.

Truth be told, I'm not following him tonight. That's done, because I'm not sure my body can take another round of his powerful finger flicks, and at this point, I don't know how far he'd take it if he caught me again. After what he did to that security guard, anything is possible. I just have to face it that he's evil. Time for a plan. Time for me to be the hero.

This is Coby Cook, signing out.

Day 6

I DAYDREAMED MY WAY THROUGH CLASSES today. Only got embarrassed once, when Mr. Laserna, my chemistry teacher, called on me to answer a question. Hearing your name when your mind is somewhere else can bring you back to reality pretty quickly, and as fear of looking stupid coursed through my veins, the fastest way I could think of to avoid his question was to start coughing. And I mean loud, rough coughing. No doubt my face turned all shades of red, and Laserna sent me into the hall to get a drink of water. By the time I returned to the room, the bell rang.

So I know what your question must be. You're wondering what I was thinking about. Honestly, finding a way to stop Zach should have been the only thing in my head, but as a plan started formulating, I couldn't help but think back to a couple years ago. Yeah, that's right. The day my dad walked out on us.

It happened late at night. Or maybe it was early in the morning. I can't remember that part so well, but I do remember my parents started arguing just after dinner, and it never seemed to let up. It was a school night, and my mom kept yelling at my dad that he needed to quiet down so I could get enough sleep for school the next day.

That just made him scream more, and I heard some loud thumps on the walls from my bedroom. I figured they were throwing things around, and I was plenty scared one of them would kill the other. Then I screamed at the top of my lungs for like fifteen seconds, and when I finished, nothing. No more yelling from them. No objects thumping into walls. I hoped it was over for the night, but as it turned out, it was really over for forever, as far as my parents were concerned.

I found out later that after I screamed, my dad sat on the edge of the bed, and my mom eventually fell asleep. She woke up a few hours later and saw a light on in the hall, and my father was no longer in bed. Turns out he must have waited until we both fell asleep, then got some of his clothes, packed them in an old suitcase, and was headed out the door when my mom found him. That's when the worst screaming and yelling started.

Probably everyone in the neighborhood heard it. Dogs started barking, and when I stepped out on the porch I could see several neighbors coming outside to see what was going on.

Getting embarrassed by Mr. Laserna in chemistry doesn't begin to rank, compared to everyone on the block watching your family implode.

The sky was dark that night. No stars or moon. Why that detail sticks with me, I'll never know. I heard Mrs. Blackford from across the street say she was going back inside to call the police. Shortly after, my father pulled away in his old Saturn Vue. That was the last time I saw him.

Mom and I went back inside, and we were both crying. She said something about having to be at work in a few hours, and how she didn't want me going to school that day or being alone, but with dad gone she couldn't afford to stay home. It was just the two of us crying and talking like that for maybe all of five minutes when the doorbell rings and it's Mrs. Hochberg.

"Charlene, I..." was all my mom could get out before Zach's mom stepped inside and wrapped my mom in a big, gentle hug. Mom started crying one of those hitching sort of cries that makes your body shake, and Mrs. Hochberg held her all the tighter.

Between tears, my mom started explaining about having to go to work and not wanting me to be alone and before I knew it, I was getting dressed to go spend the day at her house, and she would be keeping Zach home from school, too, because, "You two are best friends, and this is what best friends are for."

It might have been the best-worst day of my life. Does that even make sense?

"I'm making you boys pancakes for breakfast, my special meatball and Provolone pizza for lunch, and your favorite dessert, apple pie," Mrs. Hochberg told me on the way to her house. "I'm not sure what's for dinner yet, but you and Zach will be so busy watching your favorite superhero movies that you probably won't care."

I felt embarrassed, not from her generosity, but because I couldn't stop crying after she said it. Why should someone be so nice to me? When Zach's dad left a few years before this, I don't think I said two words to her. And as far as I knew, my mom hadn't, either.

Maybe Zach can't read minds, but it seemed like his mother could on that day. She put her arm around me as we turned up their little sidewalk leading to the porch. "I've been at this place before, Cody. So has Zach and the girls. We know what you need. We love you and want to help you through this."

The day seemed nearly perfect, all things considered. Zach and I watched old Superman, Batman, X-Men, and Spider-Man movies between meals, and promised each other to watch more over the weekend. After dinner (which ended up being fantastic, homemade tacos), when Mrs. Hochberg was slicing the pie, Katie came running into the kitchen and bumped into Alisa, who in turn stumbled into her mother. The knife accidentally give Zach's mom a nasty slash on her left index finger, and a lot of blood got on a couple pieces of pie. I have to hand it to Mrs. Hochberg. Despite all the tears and pleading for forgiveness from her daughters, she didn't show any anger at all, and after cleaning the blood off her hand and deciding stitches wouldn't be necessary, she calmed everyone down. It was pretty amazing, and I think Mrs. Hochberg may have saved me that day. I'm not really sure how, but she was there for me, even when things went wrong for her. Even now she still tells me the scar on her finger was worth it to give me a "best-worst day." That's right. Zach's mom is the one who said it first.

Still, no matter how many pieces of delicious pizza and apple pie you get to eat, the day your father walks out of your life is tough, but Mrs. Hochberg and Zach (and even his sisters) helped me get through it. They showed me such love, and except for Zach, still do. That's why the cost of my plan to stop Zach is going to be so freaking hard.

This is Coby Cook, signing out.

Day 7

I HAVE A PLAN. MAYBE IT'S NOT THE BEST plan, but it's all I've got. Will it be easy? No. But anything worthwhile often calls for hard work and sacrifice. My mom will be involved, too. There's no other way. I ran it through my head, like 50 times today. It's all for the best. I'm going to hide out under the tree in the park across from the Hochberg house tonight and wait for Zach to go off on another robbery spree. Maybe tomorrow it will all be over.

This is Coby Cook, signing out.

Day 8

THINGS WENT WELL LAST NIGHT. MRS. Hochberg and the girls seemed very surprised to find out that Zach is the ski-masked criminal, and when I informed them he'd been injured and was hiding out in the Valley National Park, they couldn't pile into their old SUV fast enough.

The park entry had a chain across the road, and we had to leave the car there. The girls brought flashlights and soon we were walking on a trail, heading towards the river.

"And how did you find out Zach is hiding here?" Mrs. Hochberg asked, her voice dry and nervous.

I'd planned my story out and fed her a line about Zach flying up to my bedroom window, telling me he didn't want to go home in case the police were able to figure out who he was, because in his struggle tonight his ski mask got ripped off his face.

"You've always been such a good friend to Zach, Coby. To all of us, actually."

"Well…" and that's all I said. I mean, I had a job ahead of me, and that's the sort of thing I didn't want to hear at a time like that.

"Hey," I said, "we still have a ways to go, and I've got some water bottles in my bookbag." I gave a bottle to Lydia, and to Katie, and to Alisa. And one last bottle to Mrs. Hochberg. It was that easy.

Later that night after my mom got home from work (actually, it was about 2 a.m. because mom had to clean a big floor of some office building), I gave her a nice cold glass of water.

This is Coby Cook, signing out.

Day 9

FIRST THING I DID THE NEXT MORNING, after drinking a couple cups of coffee (I didn't get much sleep, I was so busy!), I biked up to Zach's house. After about two straight minutes of knocking he finally opened the door. He looked terrible.

"Not sleeping well these days? Guilty conscience, perhaps?"

He turned around and shouted up the stairs. "Mom, why didn't you get the door?"

Here we go, I thought, and stepped into the house, shutting the door behind me.

"She's not here, Zach."

A blank stare zeroed in on my face, and then his eyes started opening wider. Now he seemed to be waking up.

"What did you do?" he looked a little frantic at this point, and I have to admit I enjoyed it. "Lydia," he shouted. "I swear… Katie?"

Afraid he'd react too quickly and I wouldn't be able to put the rest of my plan into action, I couldn't wait any longer. "Zach, if you ever want to see your family again, you won't lay a finger on me."

"What?" he shouted, and I think the house actually moved. Just a little.

He started reaching for me and I shoved a small box at him. He looked at me with such disdain at that moment, without even opening it. When he did, there wasn't any anger. Just tears. Lots of them.

"What did you do? How could you?

Inside the little box was a finger. With a scar on it. I'm not sure if he understood the irony behind it, but no matter.

"I want you to surrender yourself to the police, and tell them just what you've been up to. Your reign of terror has come to an end. That is, if you ever want to see your family again. If you touch me, I won't feed them. Seriously. Think about it. I'm the only one who knows where they are. Their fate is in your hands. And don't think you're going to get some leverage on me by zipping out of here and taking my mom. She's with your family. Face it, Zach. I hold all the cards. Now go to the police."

He looked like he wanted to knock me into the next state, but he wasn't that dumb. So instead he spat on me and it knocked me on my butt. It hurt more than you can imagine.

"I'm not going to the police, you idiot! I'll find them, and then you'll wish you'd never been born." He ran to the front door, smashing into it and knocking pieces into the street, then flew in the direction of my house.

The thing is, I couldn't be sure how he'd react to all of this. And I should have known he wouldn't turn himself in. After all, he's a supervillain. I picked up the box Zach dropped. Somehow the finger hadn't fallen out. Concentrating on the scar for a moment, I considered just how kind Mrs. Hochberg had always been to me.

Everything I'd need, my laptop, some water bottles, and beef jerky, were in my bookbag. I got back on my bike and pedaled a couple more blocks north and then two streets west, where I'd left Mrs. Hochberg's SUV. I wasn't a very experienced driver, but I just needed to get as far as the bus station.

That's where I am now, on a bus, headed towards Alabama. This is where I'd be even if Zach turned himself in. Because if he did, and the police got involved, things could get messy on my end. Maybe I didn't think this through as well as I should have. But heroes like me make sacrifices all the time, don't they?

This is Coby Cook, signing out.

★ ★ ★

The man powered down the battered old laptop. Energy of any kind was hard to come by, and he needed enough power for one more entry. Besides, it was difficult to see it now through all his tears. How many times had he read it from the beginning? How many times had he tried to figure out who to blame? At this point, he guessed it didn't really matter.

Yet despite all the years he'd spent lying to himself, he knew the truth. How many cities destroyed because of him? How many wars started because of him? How many millions dead because of him? No one wanted to shoulder a burden of that magnitude. But he was the catalyst that unleashed the storm known as Zach Hochberg.

He crawled out of the rubble underneath the old Hockey arena and started walking. The raggedy clothes he wore were dirty and hung poorly from his skeletal frame, but no one was there to see him, so what did it matter? When was the last time he'd eaten? Two or three days ago, probably. At least he'd found some water in the city and was able to keep his three canteens filled. He used some of the water to shave, then he trimmed his hair as best he could. In a side pocket of his bookbag he kept an old folding mirror, and on rare occasions he'd pull it out and remind himself of what his life had become.

Sometimes it was hard to remember why he currently lived under a collapsed hockey arena, but figured his poor memory had something to do with a lack of certain vitamins and nutrients in his diet. Then he'd power up his laptop if he found a working energy source or had any batteries with juice in them (sometimes he'd find an old working generator and fully charge his four batteries), and it all came flooding back when he started reading his entry at Day 1.

He turned around for a last look at home-sweet-home. He'd hidden in many places like this over the years, and didn't feel sentimental in the least. Maybe he was hesitating, just a little, about what was coming next. He sighed and trudged on.

Had he ever been to a hockey game before? Hard to remember. Sports, movies, the financial industry, and even churches, as far as he knew, hadn't existed for about two decades. All he tried to do was the right thing. But stopping Zach at any cost turned out to be far more expensive then he could have imagined. After the finger incident, it occurred to him there was no way out of it. So he left town and went into hiding. And that's when things went bad, fast. Zach, no longer caring about wearing a ski mask, escalated his crimes, but this time not to steal petty cash. The media reported about the super-powered being who was terrorizing cities, ripping apart buildings, fighting back against anyone and anything that got in his way. No one could figure out what he wanted. But Coby new.

It had to be about twelve years now since he last saw Zach face-to-face. And the first time since the finger. He was on a bicycle, traveling south at the time through Georgia. All he had were the clothes he was wearing and his laptop in a bookbag. He hadn't seen anyone else for at least two days, and no cars on the road, but by then, he probably hadn't seen any working cars in a couple years.

Out of nowhere the ground next to him seemed to explode and he was tumbling across the median, bits of gravel biting into his palms. Zach. Standing triumphant on the highway, the concrete at his feet transformed into a giant spiderweb of cracks.

"It's the Bringer of Blight himself. That's what they call you, you know. It's your supervillain name. I suppose this is where you tear me to shreds?"

Zach gave him a vacant look, almost as if he didn't realize it was Coby.

The man brushed his hands off on his shirt, got to his feet, and walked over to his former best friend. "Just do it. I'm tired of running."

"You never had my mother and sisters hidden somewhere, did you?"

Coby looked defiantly into the monster's eyes. Because of Zach's desperation and rage to find his family, his path of destruction became unstoppable, crossing borders, and even continents. For humankind, life on earth became a daily struggle to survive.

"Answer me," Zach said. He didn't shout it or look threatening or flick Coby with his fingers. He almost sounded disinterested, which frightened Coby more than anything else.

"Okay." Coby had to look away for a moment and gather his thoughts…what he assumed would be his last thoughts. But he was the hero, the good guy, so he needed to look Zach in the eye once more. "It was the only way to have any power over you, to make you stop before you killed someone or committed a crime so big that the freaking Army would be coming after you." Zach continued gazing back at him with no change in his expression. "There was no way I'd be able to hide them all and feed them, because you'd just follow me and get them back. Then I wouldn't have any leverage. So I killed them. The night before I gave you the finger, literally. Your mother and sisters and my mother too. It didn't bother me as much as you might think, because someone had to be the good guy and find a way to stop you, and like a true hero, I was willing to do whatever it took, at any cost, to put a stop to you."

Tears were welling in Zach's eyes and Coby realized that his nemesis might actually have some real human feelings left in his bones.

"I never stole much, just enough to help my family," Zach said, his voice hitching a little, and Coby thought he might break down right in front of him. "Mom was getting behind on the bills, and I found an easy way to help out. I never would have let it go too far if you'd have just left us alone."

Zach's face was red and wet, and Coby started feeling embarrassed for this horrible man who'd changed life on earth forever.

"But you did go too far. You put a man in a coma."

"You're no better than me, Coby Cook. You're a murderer. You're probably sicker than me."

But Coby knew this wasn't true. Zach's the real monster, he told himself. Coby was Batman to Zach's Joker.

"Staying alive is the best way for you to pay for your share of the sins we committed," Zach said, then jumped into the sky and flew out of sight before Coby could blink.

Funny how that chance meeting so many years ago came to mind now. He hadn't seen or even heard anything about Zach since that day. Then again, it wasn't like he could turn on cable news or look it up on the internet.

With a few more steps he entered the shadow of the largest remaining building in Chicago. How it was still standing, he couldn't figure, but he was thankful it was there. More than likely there wouldn't be any power for the elevator, but walking up the stairs would be cathartic.

The ascent turned out to be more difficult than he thought it would be. Several times he sat to rest, and it didn't take long before he'd finished off the water in his canteen. Sixteen more flights to the roof. And then one last journal entry to write.

Day 7316

Perhaps the loneliness is the worst part.

I haven't seen another human being for close to three years now. Early on, when I first went on the run and it was kind of exciting, people were everywhere.

I blended in as best I could, moving from city to city, trying to avoid Zach. I never felt lonely during the first couple years. But when Zach stepped it up and tore apart cities, states, and even countries in the search for his family, people went into hiding. Farmers didn't work their fields, crops started dying out, and hence Zach's supervillain name, the Bringer of Blight.

The guy could fly anywhere he wanted, and so fast. But the attacks were completely random. One moment he'd be in Delaware, moving at lightning speed, pulling apart buildings with his bare hands, and the next hour he'd be sighted in some other country, across the Atlantic, doing the same. I'm not so sure that Zach thought I had the resources to move his mother and sisters out of the country, though. My best guess is that he was so enraged with me he'd just fly for a while, land, and start destroying whatever was in front of him.

Is Zach Hochberg still alive? Does it really matter anymore? But if he's dead, I can't begin to guess how he died, because military forces around the world hit him with their most powerful non-nuclear weapons and didn't so much as scratch him.

Nearly finished now. My battery is getting low and I'm tired. Tired of writing, tired of running, tired of always being hungry. And most of all tired of remembering when I reread this stupid journal. But I have a confession to make. I've always been jealous that Zach can fly. Sure, I was afraid the one time he grabbed me and flew me across town, but that was on his terms. A bad guy isn't supposed to be granted powers like that. It should have been me…it should have been me. So as I sit and write these words on the roof of the tallest building I could find, I'm going to let you in on one last secret. Now it's my turn to fly. On my terms.

This is Coby Cook, signing out.

THE END

W.H.ROBINSON.
IN SEARCH OF ELDORADO

ELDORADO

Gaily bedight,
  A gallant knight,
In sunshine and in shadow,
  Had journeyed long,
  Singing a song,
In search of Eldorado.

  But he grew old—
  This knight so bold—
And o'er his heart a shadow—
  Fell as he found
  No spot of ground
That looked like Eldorado.

  And, as his strength
  Failed him at length,
He met a pilgrim shadow—
  'Shadow,' said he,
  'Where can it be—
This land of Eldorado?'

  'Over the Mountains
  Of the Moon,
Down the Valley of the Shadow,
  Ride, boldly ride,'
  The shade replied,—
'If you seek for Eldorado!'

— Edgar Allan Poe, 1849

QUEEN OF THE SAGEBRUSH FRONTIER
FIREHAIR
by JOHN STARR
AND THE SEASONS BLOSSOMED AND FADED... AND THE MAIDEN CALLED Firehair DWELT ON WITH THE DAKOTA NATION... AND OFTEN SHE STARED AT THE STAR-STUDDED SKY AND PONDERED THE RIDDLE AS TO WHO SHE WAS AND FROM WHENCE SHE CAME...
...BUT THOUGH HER SKIN WAS WHITE, HER WAYS WERE THOSE OF HER RED-SKINNED BROTHERS.
GO NOT FAR FROM OUR FIRES, FIREHAIR, FOR SOON WE START ON THE BUFFALO HUNT.
I WILL LOOK TO MY TRAPS, TEHAMA, BUT I WILL RETURN IN TIME TO RIDE WITH YOU.
1

AH, SHE COMES! FOR HER SCALP, FINGERS HAS PROMISED ME A LONG RIFLE AND MUCH FIREWATER!

BUT THE CUBS WOULD TELL IF I KILLED HER. IT IS BETTER THAT I RIDE TO HIM WITH THE NEWS THAT SHE GOES WITH THE WARRIORS TO HUNT THE BUFFALO.
SOON.
MY SNARE IS EMPTY BUT PERHAPS THE BEAVER WAS NOT SO WARY. WAIT FOR ME HERE, LITTLE ONES!

SEE SISTER, IT IS THUS THE FOOLISH CATAMOUNT IS CAUGHT.
BE CAREFUL, BROTHER, OR WHEN FIREHAIR RETURNS SHE WILL PULL YOUR EARS
At THAT SECOND.

FIREHAIR - FIREHAIR - HELP - HELP!

AH, LITTLE AX'S EYES WILL BURN WITH JEALOUSY WHEN I SHOW HIM THIS SKIN! HARK, THOSE SCREAMS!
CRIES FROM THE CLEARING... THE YOUNG ONES!
...S AHEAD... SUDDENLY A TAWNY FORM FLASHES TOWARD THE HELPLESS BOY!
HOOFS LASH... THEN THE GREAT CAT SPRINGS.
BUT WITH A SQUEAL OF RAGE THE HORSE, DEVIL-EYE, WHIRLS.
A CATAMOUNT ON DEVIL-EYE... WING TRUE, O TOMAHAWK!

LATER.
THERE COME THE SCOUTS I SENT TO SEEK OUT THE BUFFALO HERD.
LO_ AND YONDER COMES THE FIREHAIR ONE FROM HER TRAPS.

SHE KILLED IT, BUT IT WOULD NOT HAVE COME IF I HAD NOT TESTED THE SNARE!

HO, CHIEF TEHAMA, BUFFALO HERD IS MANY HANDS BIG. EVEN NOW IT ENTERS THE VALLEY.
COME WARRIORS, MAKE READY FOR THE KILL!

TAKE CARE, FIREHAIR_ SHOOT NOT THIS ONE WITH THE GOLDEN HORNS IF YOU WOULD NOT HAVE LITTLE AX DEPART FOR THE HAPPY HUNTING GROUNDS.
FEAR NOT, LITTLE AX_ GO WITH YOUR STALKERS. I RIDE WITH THE HUNTERS

LATER...
LOOK _ THERE'S THE SIGNAL _ THE STALKERS HAVE STARTED TOWARD THE HERD.

SOFTLY_ CREEP SOFTLY LEST THEY STAMPEDE BEFORE WE ARE CLOSE ENOUGH TO TURN THEM TOWARD THE HUNTERS!

RANGERS COMICS

WYLE
Firehair WAITED WITH CHIEF TEHAMA AND HIS WARRIORS IN A HIDDEN RAVINE, LITTLE AX AND THE STALKERS CREPT EVER CLOSER TO THE GRAZING HERD. Then SUDDENLY THEIR BUFFALO ROBES WERE WHIPPED OFF AND... AND...

NOW_NOW_ MAKE PLENTY NOISE!
STAMPEDE START_ KEEP THEM HEADED TOWARD THE VALLEY! SEE_ OUR HUNTERS RIDE TO CUT THEM DOWN.

RIDE_RIDE! KILL_KILL!

DIE, KING OF THE PLAINS_IT IS FROM YOUR FLESH THE DAKOTA NATION HAS LONG TAKEN ITS STRENGTH AND COURAGE!

BUT ON A NEARBY HILL,
THIS HERE'S A GOOD SPOT, BLACKIE_ THE VARMINT'LL PASS BELOW US.

WE'RE IN LUCK_ SHE'S SEPARATED FROM THE OTHERS_ YOU TAKE THE HORSE_I'LL TAKE HER.
SAY THE WORD, FINGERS_I'M READY!
6

AH, FIREHAIR'S SPEAR STRIKES TRUE_ ALREADY SHE HAS KILLED A FULL HAND OF THEM_ WHY_ WHAT MAKES THAT GLINT BEHIND HER ON THE BLUFF?

NOW, BLACKIE, SHOOT!
OKAY, BOSS!

And AS THE GUNS BARK THEIR DEATH SONG...

IT WAS AN AMBUSH_ SOMEONE SHOT HER_ I SAW THE RIFLE SMOKE!

BUFFALO GONE FEAR-CRAZY_ WILL TRAMPLE HER_ THERE IS BUT ONE WAY!

AND CHANTING THE DAKOTA WAR SONG LITTLE AX SPLITS THE THUNDERING HERD.
7

Minutes LATER
YES, FATHER, I HAVE THE KEY. I'LL KEEP IT ON A STRING AROUND MY NECK!
SHE LIVES_ SHE SPEAKS_ BUT HER WORDS I DO NOT UNDERSTAND.

FIREHAIR_ IT IS YOUR LITTLE BROTHER_ DO YOU NOT KNOW ME?
I'LL BE YOUR PRINCESS, FATHER AND THE WAGON IS OUR PUMPKIN COACH.

LITTLE AX_ AH NOW I REMEMBER EVERYTHING_ MY FATHER_ THE MASSACRE_ MY LIFE WITH YOUR PEOPLE_ BUT WHY DID I FALL?
SOMEONE WAS HIDING IN THE HILLS_ THEY FIRED AT YOU!

SEE_ A BULLET RAKED DEVIL-EYE'S FLANK. WHEN HE FELL THE BULLET MEANT FOR YOU WENT WIDE. BUT WHERE GO YOU NOW?
TO FIND WHO THEY WERE AND WHY THEY WANTED TO KILL ME.

WAIT, WAIT_ YOU MUST NOT GO ALONE_ WAIT!

Later.
I TRIED TO STOP HER BUT SHE WOULD NOT LISTEN. I SAW HER PICK UP THE TRAIL.
DAKOTA BRAVES, FOLLOW ME FOR FIREHAIR IS OF OUR PEOPLE AND HER FIGHT IS OUR FIGHT!
8

But ahead.
SO HERE THE TRAIL ENDS... THEN THAT MUST BE THE KILLERS' DEN.

NOW I KNOW... IT WAS AFTER THE MASSACRE... HE'S THE MAN WHO BENT OVER ME... TOUCHED ME WITH THAT CRIPPLED HAND... THE HAND THAT HAUNTED MY DREAMS!

AND INSIDE...
...AND THAT'S HOW BLACKIE AND ME KILLED THE WENCH. SHE WAS THE ONLY ONE WHO COULD HAVE PINNED THE RAID ON US.
SHE'LL MAKE US RICH, EH FINGERS?

YEAH, I'LL SAY! I KNOW A DANCEHALL GIRL WHO CAN TAKE HER PLACE AND WE'LL HIRE AN EASTERN LAWYER TO PUT IN A CLAIM FOR THE ESTATE. WHAT!

DROP YOUR GUNS!

IT'S HER... THE RED HEADED DEVIL... KILL HER!

Then RAGES A DEADLY DUEL.

GOOD WORK, BLACKIE... YOU GOT HER!

BUT.
REDSKINS... THEY GOT FINGERS... WE'RE TRAPPED... DON'T KILL US... DON'T KILL US!

HUH... LIKE SQUAWS THEY BEG FOR MERCY... BUT IF THE FIREHAIR ONE IS HARMED, WE KILL!
SHE LIVES, TEHAMA... SHE LIVES!

LATER.
HERE, FIREHAIR, THIS IS YOURS. NOW PERHAPS YOU FORGET YOUR RED BROTHERS AND GO TO YOUR PEOPLE.
I... I'M NOT SURE, CHIEF. I WILL WAIT UNTIL THE HARVEST MOON CROSSES THE SKY BEFORE I DECIDE WHAT TO DO.

GENE TUNNEY
UNDEFEATED HEAVYWEIGHT CHAMPION OF THE GOLDEN AGE OF SPORT.....

ALTHOUGH THE FIGHTING MARINE RAN UP A STRING OF THIRTY KNOCKOUTS IN HIS FIRST THIRTY-FIVE BOUTS...GENE SOON FOUND HE HAD BRITTLE HANDS...SO IN 1921 HE TOOK TO THE WOODS AND CURED HIS DAMAGED MITTS....

A YEAR OF THIS.... AN I'LL BE ABLE TO BELT A STEAM-ENGINE!

AFTER KNOCKING-OFF THE CONTENDERS HE FINALLY GOT A SHOT AT DEMPSEY'S CROWN. WHILE IN TRAINING IT WAS LEARNED THAT GENE WAS A LOVER OF SHAKESPEARE AND FINE BOOKS! TUNNEY WASN'T GIVEN A CHANCE WITH THE MANASSA MAULER ...BUT TO EVERYONES SURPRISE HE EXPERTLY OUTBOXED THE CHAMP AND WON THE TITLE!

IT'S IN TH' BAG F'R TH' CHAMP...

TH' BUM IS READIN' SHAKIN-SPEERS!

1927 BROUGHT THE FAMOUS $2,500,000 GATE AND THE "LONG-COUNT". DOWNED FOR THE FIRST TIME IN HIS CAREER, GENE RECOVERED AT THE COUNT OF NINE (SOME THOUGHT IT WAS AN EASY 12!) AND WENT ON TO TAKE THE DECISION FROM DEMPSEY

ONE, TWO... BUTTON MY SHOE... ER THREE, FOUR...

HAVE YOU GOT A SANDWICH?

TO RETIRE OR NOT TO RETIRE... THAT IS THE QUESTION?

AFTER KNOCKING OUT TOM HEENEY IN 1928, THE FIGHTING MARINE RETIRED AS UNDEFEATED HEAVYWEIGHT CHAMPION OF THE WORLD

LEGENDARIUM

BY MICHAEL BUNKER & KEVIN G. SUMMERS

CHAPTER FIVE
THE PUGILIST

Bombo was the first to his feet. He staggered across the debris that now covered every square inch of the escape pod, and finally reached the door.

"Wait!" Alistair said.

"Wait for what?"

Alistair climbed to his feet and dusted himself off. "What's the plan?"

"I plan to open this hatch," Bombo said.

"But you don't know what might be out there," Alistair said. "Maybe we crash-landed on the Mome Wraiths' home planet or something."

Bombo smirked at Alistair. "You know I love you, right?"

Alistair scowled. "Of course not."

"Exactly," Bombo said. "So then you'll understand why I'm going to open this hatch no matter what's out there." He pulled a lever and blew open the escape hatch. There was a hissing noise as the pressurized air of the vessel whooshed into the atmosphere outside. Bombo was relieved, and a little nervous, when he saw the white light that signified their passage into another world.

"Foley," he said, "come on, let's get out of here."

The creative writing teacher was now standing with his back against the wall of the escape pod. He was breathing dramatically in through his nose and out through his mouth.

"What in the world are you doing?" Bombo said.

"Hyperventilating," said Alistair.

"We don't have time for that."

"You're telling me!" Alistair wheezed with each word, and it took every bit of willpower Bombo had not to grab the great fool by the shoulders and shake him. But that would probably just make the situation worse.

"There's another world being threatened," Bombo said. "Maybe we can save this one."

"And maybe we can let it die, just like *Beyond the Stars!*" said Alistair. "Who knows what kind of changes have occurred to the timeline now? And it's all our fault!"

Bombo grabbed the smaller man by the scruff of the neck and dragged him toward the hatch. "There's nothing we can do about that now," he shouted. "But if we stand around here doing nothing, even worse things might happen."

"But—"

Bombo slapped Alistair across the face. Alistair's mouth fell open, and tears welled in his eyes. "I can't believe you did that," he said, shocked. "No one has ever slapped me before."

"Too bad," Bombo said. "Maybe if someone had taken the time to scold you once in a while you wouldn't be such a prig. Now come on, we have a world to save."

"Fine," Alistair said, "but if you ever hit me again, I'm going to take you down."

"You could try," Bombo said. "Besides, I could probably use a smack now and then too."

The writers stepped through the light and emerged inside a poorly lit saloon. The walls were brick, the floorboards scuffed and worn, and there wasn't a single window in the place. An oak bar dominated one corner of the room, and pub tables filled every available space. The place was filled with people, all laughing and carrying on, blissfully unaware that their universe was on the verge of extinction.

The first thing Bombo noticed as he stepped into the saloon was Alistair's clothing. Only a moment before he'd been dressed in the dark blue coveralls of the *Alamo-02* space station, but now he wore a brown suit that looked like something out of the 1920's. Bombo looked down at his own clothes and found he was wearing a gray suit of similar design. "I don't know how the Legendarium works," he whispered, "but I like these threads a lot better than the last ones."

"Just wait until we find out that we're trapped in an F. Scott Fitzgerald story," Alistair said. "Or James Joyce. Maybe the world would be a better place if we let a few of those snoozers wink out of existence."

"You have to be kidding me," Bombo said.

"Do I look like I'm kidding?"

"No. You look like an idiot, and your words confirm the theory."

"Hey, you two," said a huge man in a black suit. "Are you here to drink or run your mouths?"

"Definitely drink," Bombo said.

"Um, drink?" said Alistair.

"Bar's that way," said the huge man. His hair was close-cropped, and as far as Alistair could tell, he had no neck.

They waded through the crowd and approached the bar. "I'll take a beer," Bombo said, "and my friend here will have…"

"A glass of white wine," said Alistair. "Something with nice mouthfeel."

The bartender looked at him with derision. "Very funny," he said. "We have moonshine. You can have it straight, on the rocks, or in a cocktail. I'd suggest the cocktail, unless you like the taste of gasoline."

"Moonshine?" Alistair said.

"Oh," Bombo said, realizing that they'd just stepped into the era of prohibition. "We'll take two cocktails," he said. "Whatever you think is likely to taste the least like gasoline. Thanks."

When the bartender turned away, Bombo leaned over to Alistair and whispered, "Prohibition! Isn't this cool?"

Alistair shook his head. "If you find a Tommy gun please shoot me in the face."

"Oh man, this just gets better and better," Bombo said with a smile.

The bartender set about making their drinks as Bombo explained to Alistair what he'd deduced about their situation. Given the time period, Alistair's earlier remarks about the possible author of this story now seemed highly likely. "This is the Jazz Age," Bombo said. "We're probably dealing with a member of the Lost Generation," he said. "Maybe if we could figure out our exact location, that would give us an indication of what we're dealing with."

They looked all around, but the walls were bare. Very likely this speakeasy was in the basement of another establishment, a business that was run merely as a front for the saloon.

"Here you go," said the bartender. He handed them their cocktails. "That'll be two dollars."

Bombo and Alistair exchanged a look. They had only the clothes on their backs and the cash in their wallets—which was going to be in modern bills. Alistair reached into the pocket of his trousers and took out his billfold. He removed two crisp dollars and was amazed to see that they were both dated 1925.

"Here you go," Alistair said. "Thank you."

The bartender looked at him with disgust. It wasn't until they found a table in a corner of the saloon that Alistair realized he'd forgotten to give the man a tip.

"Do you recognize this bar?" Bombo said. "I've read a lot of literature from this period, but it doesn't ring a bell."

"Not at all," Alistair said.

"It's not Paris or Spain from what I can tell, what with it being prohibition and all."

Alistair just grunted and held up his drink in a mock toast.

They sipped their cocktails and sat amid the din and activity of the other drinkers. Bombo found himself watching a man and a woman sitting at the next table. The man had dark hair and thick eyebrows, a mustache and a square jaw. He had cauliflower ears and a crooked nose and a twinkle in his eyes and a five o'clock shadow. He was a man's man—anyone could see it. The woman was a blonde, with full, pouty lips and a figure shaped like an hourglass. She was clearly drunk, her voice rising and falling as she spoke. Bombo and Alistair listened closely, hoping that fate, luck, providence, or whatever it was that was steering them through the Legendarium would once again guide their steps.

"I can't believe you would do this to me," the blonde bombshell said. "It's like you don't care at all about how I feel."

The man quaffed a cocktail in one manly gulp and banged the glass down on the table. "It doesn't matter how you feel," he said. "I'm gonna win the fight and that's that."

"But what if you lose?" she said.

"I won't," he said.

"But what if you do?" she said.

"Woman," he said, "that isn't going to happen, so you don't need to worry about it."

"Oh my God," Bombo said. His eyes had a faraway glassy look as his memory registered what was happening. "This is Hemingway."

Alistair's eyes widened. "That dreadful man is Ernest Hemingway?"

"No," Bombo said. "This is his first novel: *The Pugilist.*"

"I've never even heard of it," Alistair said, and took another sip from his cocktail.

"No, I don't believe you would have," Bombo replied. "You'd have to have even a cursory knowledge of literature and history, coupled with a love for the written word."

"Stuff it, Dawson," Alistair sneered.

"I just can't believe you would treat me like I'm your *property*," said the blonde. She took a sip of her cocktail.

The man shrugged. "Don't you worry your pretty little head about it," he said. "Everything is going to turn out fine." And with that, he stood, hoisted the woman to her feet, and kissed her.

"He seems like a real asshole," Alistair said.

"He's a man's man," said Bombo.

"I can't stand Hemingway," Alistair said. "O-ver-rated."

"You have just cemented your position as the worst literature critic in the history of the world, Alistair. Did your mother have any kids that lived?"

"It doesn't matter," Alistair said, waving his hand. "What happens in this story?"

"That guy is Jack Walcott," Bombo said. "He's a boxer."

"That sounds like a Hemingway story," Alistair said.

"The woman is his lover, Agnes. Jack owes a lot of money to a man named Danny Hogan. Danny is another boxer. He owns a gymnasium in New Jersey."

"Let me guess," Alistair said. "Jack bets a night with Agnes that he can beat Danny in a boxing match."

"Right," Bombo said. "I thought you didn't know this story."

"I hate Ernest Hemingway," Alistair said.

"What books *do* you like?" Bombo asked.

"I really enjoyed the Harry Potter series," Alistair said. "I gave all of those five stars."

Bombo just stared at Alistair and blinked. He couldn't think of anything appropriate to say.

"This story is appalling," Alistair said. "Maybe we should just let it go."

"How can you say that after what we just went through?"

Alistair took a sip of his drink. He was beginning to appreciate the faint gasoline flavor in the beverage. "I know, I know… you're right," he said. "But what are we supposed to do here? Are we still looking for the vorpal sword, or was it lost on the space station?"

"I don't know," Bombo said. "We just need to keep our eyes open and act whenever it seems like the story is about to go off the tracks."

"What happens next?" Alistair asked.

"The fight," Bombo said. "Jack and Agnes are probably on their way to the gym right now. We should go."

The writers finished their drinks and followed Hemingway's protagonist out of the saloon. They tailed the boxer and his girl through the filthy streets of Jersey City, occasionally having to step over or around an unconscious wino as the lights of Manhattan glowed in the distance. Before long, they came to an ancient gymnasium with a sign overhead that read:

THE HEALTH FARM

A bouncer stopped them when they reached the front door. He appeared to be the identical twin of the bouncer at the speakeasy.

"Five dollars each for admission," he said. His voice was thick and slow. He was a no-nonsense fellow who'd seen his share of troubles.

Alistair reached into his wallet and produced a ten-dollar bill. Once again, the Legendarium had provided exactly what they needed, exactly when they needed it. How it was able to do this, and yet was seemingly incapable of protecting its stories from destruction, was a mystery to Alistair.

The writers slipped into the gymnasium and were immediately overwhelmed by the aroma of sweat and greed and broken dreams. Half a hundred men in working-class clothes were jammed into the small space. A throng they were—a hive mind buzzing with hopeless activity. They were crowded around a boxing ring that dominated the room like an altar in the high church of despair. The purpose of this fight, for the audience in any case, was to offer something, *anything*, upon which they could gamble. It was a frantic grasp at a solitary instant of hope… hope that lightning might strike and the sun would shine on them for a moment. Like all such worshipers, the men peered up at the altar with prayerful eyes. They would have bet on anything—turtle races, dog fighting, whatever—but two men knocking one another senseless was the main event of this particular evening.

"Who wins the fight?" Alistair asked.

"Danny Hogan," Bombo said.

"He gets the girl for the night?"

"Yeah. She leaves Jack standing in the locker room with a broken heart and ten grand in debt."

"Is that the end of the story?" Alistair asked.

"No. Jack hangs himself from the rafters," Bombo said.

"That's terrible," Alistair said.

"It's Hemingway," said Bombo. "It is what it is."

"I hate Hemingway," Alistair said.

"I'm pretty sure he wouldn't care much for you either," Bombo replied, "but who could say, considering you've never published anything."

"You're a real peach," Alistair said.

The lights dimmed then, and a skinny man in a black suit climbed into the ring. He raised a bullhorn to his lips and spoke.

"Ladies and gentlemen!" he said. "This fight is scheduled for ten rounds. Introducing first, in the black trunks… Danny Hogan!"

A man in a black bathrobe appeared out of the locker room. He had thinning hair and a scowl permanently fixed upon his face. He walked slowly to the ring, his eyes darting all around as if he expected someone in the crowd to jump at any moment. Boos and catcalls filled the gymnasium.

"You know what I like?" Alistair said.

"What do you like?" said Bombo.

"Professional wrestling," Alistair said.

Bombo gave Alistair the long, slow blink again.

"Professional wrestlers are at least as athletic as participants in any other sport, and since the stories are plotted out in advance, they almost always put on a good show."

"It's fake," Bombo said. "You do know it's fake, right?"

"Of course I do," Alistair said. "Don't be silly. That's the point. *Because* it's fake, I don't have to feel guilty about them actually hurting one another. It's all just great fun."

"Have you ever looked at the statistics on dead wrestlers?" said Bombo. "It's like the most dangerous entertainment there is, other than maybe… I don't know… bullfighting or something."

"Shhh," Alistair said. "He's going to announce the other guy."

"And now," said the announcer, "his opponent, in blue trunks… Jack Walcott!"

There were cheers and wolf whistles, but Jack didn't show up immediately. The announcer said his name again, and after a few long moments, the man from the speakeasy appeared in the entryway that led from the locker room. He wore a white bathrobe and had a cocky smile plastered on his face. His girlfriend darted out from the locker room several seconds later. She looked like she'd been crying.

"Maybe I should go after her," Alistair said.

"And miss the fight?" asked Bombo.

"She might be the cornerstone of this whole story," said Alistair.

"This is Hemingway," said Bombo. "I kind of doubt it, but whatever you think is best. Say, do you think they have any concessions? I'm starving. Bring me back a hot dog, will you, precious?"

Alistair disappeared after Agnes while Bombo settled back in his seat to watch the fight. A referee climbed through the ropes and called the two fighters to the center of the ring. They touched gloves in a show of sportsmanship as the referee explained the rules of the fight. He wanted a fair fight. He wanted them to observe the rules of boxing and sportsmanship and civility. He wanted them to put on a good show. He dismissed the boxers to their respective corners so they could pray or make peace with God or whatever.

A concession vendor walked past, and Bombo ordered a Coke and a bag of popcorn. He had just enough money in his wallet to pay the tab. He was still full of the vain hope that Foley would return with a hot dog, but he wanted to tide himself over until then. He munched nervously as the bell rang and the boxers darted back to the middle of the ring.

AGNES RAN OUT A SIDE DOOR OF THE Health Farm and was pacing up and down in the alley smoking a cigarette when Alistair found her.

"Excuse me, ma'am," he said. "I couldn't help but notice that you were crying."

"Mind your own business, creep," Agnes snapped. Her mascara ran down her face in grayish streaks. She turned from Alistair, hiding her face.

"I'm sorry," Alistair said. "It's just that—I overheard your conversation with your boyfriend at the speakeasy. I know about the bet."

Agnes bowed her head and cried. "How can he treat me like that?" she asked. "I've been good to him. I stood by him when everyone else thought he was a loser."

"I know," Alistair said. "It makes me sick to think he could treat you that way."

"It's like he doesn't respect me at all. He treats me like a dog."

"You shouldn't put up with that kind of behavior," Alistair said. "You deserve better."

Agnes was angry now. She wiped away her tears, further streaking her mascara. "You're right," she said. "I'm not going to let him use me as a wager. I don't belong to that bastard! I could get another man just like that." She snapped her fingers and nodded before taking a puff from her dwindling cigarette.

"That's right," Alistair said. "You're beautiful and smart and obviously loyal to a fault."

"What's that supposed to mean?" said Agnes. She was in a feisty mood now.

"Nothing," Alistair said. "So, what are you going to do?"

"I'm getting out of here," Agnes said. "If you see Jack, tell him to forget he ever knew me. Which may not be all that hard after he gets his head caved in tonight."

"I'll do just that," Alistair said. He smiled as he watched her walk away. She was a gorgeous broad, a woman any man would kill for.

Agnes reached the end of the alley and stepped out into the street.

Broad? Alistair thought. *Where the hell did that come from?* It was then, when it was too late, that he realized—to his horror—that his job here was *not* to save the dame from her abusive boyfriend. Rather, his mission was to see that this story unfolded in the way that Ernest Hemingway had originally intended. If Agnes walked out of the story, any number of things might happen, but most of them were bad.

"Wait!" Alistair shouted, but the damage was done. As Agnes stepped into the street, she turned at Alistair's call. A white delivery truck was speeding down the street and she never saw it. She was killed instantly.

"No!" Alistair screamed. He ran to her, but as he ran, the bricks that formed the alley floor crumbled beneath his feet and transformed into quicksand. In a flash, he was sinking. As he sensed death approaching, he looked back down the alley and noticed the looming black shadows all around him.

Mome wraiths.

BOMBO WAS ON HIS FEET, CHEERING wildly as Jack landed two quick lefts into Danny Hogan's face. The man in the black trunks staggered backward as Jack Walcott pressed his attack. He landed left after left on Danny's head and shoulders. Finally, the owner of the gymnasium reeled and lowered his guard, and Jack connected a punch squarely on his jaw.

Danny went down like a sack of feed and the referee began to count.

In the crowd, Bombo's eyes narrowed as he realized that something was wrong. "This isn't how this was supposed to happen," he said aloud.

"No," said a sad voice, "it's not."

Bombo turned to see an old man with a bushy white beard sitting beside him. He wore a plain suit and a sweater vest. Bombo would have recognized the man anywhere.

It was Ernest Hemingway.

In the ring, the referee was signaling the timekeeper to ring the bell.

"Sir?" Bombo slid closer to the old man. "What's happening?"

"You're friend broke my story," Hemingway said.

"He's not my—what? What happened?"

"He talked Agnes into walking out on Jack. Now she's dead, and this world is collapsing."

"Alistair!" Bombo said. His anger was tempered only by his own sadness. "He destroyed your first novel… I—I don't know what to say."

"Ladies and gentlemen," said the announcer through his bullhorn, "the winner of this bout, by knockout: Jack Walcott!"

"That's not all," Hemingway said. "Do you know how I died?"

"Liver cancer brought on by hemochromatosis," Bombo said. "You died in 1971. I remember—"

"No." Hemingway's eyes were full of despair. "I never saw those last ten years. I took my own life in 1961."

"What? No. I remember…"

Danny Hogan was still lying flat on his back. The referee and the announcer were checking on him, but it was evident to Bombo that something was wrong. The man hadn't moved an inch since he'd collapsed.

"He's dead," Hemingway said. "Jack killed him with that last punch. I almost had the story end this way, but I thought my other ending was more powerful. I thought it displayed more of the human condition."

Bombo rubbed his temples as a terrible pain throbbed in his head.

"Your brain is being recoded," said the old man known as Papa. "Information that you've been storing for years is being overwritten."

"What do you mean?"

"In the *new* now, the manuscript for this novel, *The Pugilist*, was lost when my first wife decided to pack all of my work into a suitcase and hop on a train to meet me in Geneva. She left the suitcase on the train… and *The Pugilist* was gone forever."

"Your first novel—" Bombo began.

"—was *The Torrents of Spring*," Hemingway said. "I managed to rework some of this material into another story, but this—this perfect first novel—it died."

"I'm going to *kill* Alistair," Bombo said.

"No. You need him," Hemingway said. A depression had settled on the man, one that would never really leave him. "Neither one of you alone can save the Legendarium."

"I'm so sorry," Bombo said. "About what happened to you."

"There's one more thing," said Hemingway. "Remember how Cuba became the fifty-first state in 1959?"

"Oh, no."

Hemingway nodded sadly. "Batista and his cronies were overthrown by communists and we've been in a pissing contest with them ever since. Almost caused a nuclear war, but at least we managed not to bomb the human race into oblivion."

Bombo was speechless. His mouth hung open and tears formed in his eyes.

Bellows

"A thousand-thousand other changes happened too," Hemingway said. "For example, how'd you get the name *Bombo?*"

"Don't tell me…"

"I have to tell you, young man, so buck up and listen or I'll cuff you one on the ear," Hemingway said. "Roberto Clemente, the great Puerto Rican outfielder for the Pittsburgh Pirates, was in Havana when that city fell on New Year's Eve in 1958. The next morning, on New Year's Day of 1959, Clemente saw so many of the poor and needy flooding the streets of Havana that he pledged his life to ease human suffering. That, in and of itself, was a good thing. But every change ripples through time and changes other things."

"No…" Bombo said. "He tried to clasp his hands over his ears, but Hemingway, still strong and fiery, wrestled Bombo's hands down again.

"Roberto Clemente was killed flying relief supplies to earthquake-stricken Nicaragua in 1972."

"Oh my…" Bombo said, "Not Clemente! He was my favorite player growing up! Him and another great Puerto Rican player: Bombo Rivera. In fact, my mother nicknamed me after Bombo."

Hemingway looked into Bombo's eyes. "Now you see."

"Bombo took up baseball because he idolized Roberto Clemente. They played together for several years after Clemente got the Pirates to trade for Bombo in 1976. In fact, they were neck-and-neck for MVP in '78."

Hemingway shook his head. "Nope. Now none of that ever happened. Bombo Rivera got to play a few seasons in the majors, but with Clemente dead, he was never traded to the Pirates. He never was mentored by Clemente. Bombo spent most of his career in the minor leagues. He's more famous for his name than for anything he ever did in the game."

Bombo was still shaking his head. He couldn't believe that in the new world, no one would even know why he was nicknamed Bombo.

"It's all true," Ernest said. "It's all the *new* truth."

"I can't believe Clemente died in '72," Bombo said.

Hemingway exhaled. "Yes, he died when you were just a boy. It's not just *some*thing that changes when a literary world dies. *Every*thing changes."

"This is a disaster," Bombo said. "An absolute disaster. Is there anything we can do to fix the situation?"

"The best you can do is to not let it happen again," Hemingway said. "Half the world has read the Wonderland books. If those disappear, anything could happen. You could even lose your wife."

"Okay," Bombo said. "Fine. What should I do right now?"

"Your friend is outside drowning in quicksand," said Hemingway. "You might want to help him. *I'd* do it, but I think I'd probably knock the son of a bitch out cold if I saw him."

"He's not my friend," Bombo said.

"Whatever," said Ernest Hemingway.

★ ★ ★

As Bombo left the Health Farm he noticed the living shadows descending from every corner of the gymnasium. The Mome Wraiths were here, devouring all life, and soon this world would cease to exist, just like the science fiction world created by Russell Benjamin.

Bombo pushed through the crowd and toward the side door through which he'd seen Alistair depart in search of Agnes. He stepped through the doorway and nearly toppled into the quicksand that consumed the city beyond. Tall buildings were sinking in the sand, and as they leaned they crumbled and collapsed. Overhead, the sky was black with Mome Wraiths, and their screeching filled the air with a hellish din.

"Help!" Alistair screamed.

Bombo looked down and saw his partner and nemesis almost completely submerged. He had one hand out, grasping for a lifeline, for anything to save him from the pull of the sand. *I'm the lifeline*, Bombo realized. He lay down flat on his stomach and stretched his upper body over the quicksand. His hand brushed Alistair's fingertips, but he couldn't—quite—reach him.

"Your… shirt," Alistair gasped. The quicksand had reached to the bottom of his lip.

Bombo removed his flannel shirt—strangely he was wearing it again now, and the gray suit was gone—and rolled it up tight. He tossed one end to Alistair, who grabbed it and held on for dear life.

The bearded author pulled with all his might and managed to yank Alistair out of the sand and into the relative safety of the doorway. The two sat there, panting, while living shadows consumed the gymnasium to one side of them and a city collapsed on the other.

"Agnes is dead," Alistair said. "I don't know what I was thinking. I talked her into leaving Jack."

"You don't know the half of it," Bombo said. "You really screwed up this time."

"I know," Alistair said. "I know."

"How are we going to get out of here?" Bombo asked.

"I was hoping you had a plan."

"Well, we can't go outside," Bombo said. He looked around. "If there's a doorway to another story or back to the Legendarium, it must be inside the gym. Come on then, let's find it."

They stood and entered once more into the Health Farm. Mome Wraiths had devoured nearly everything, but an old man with a white beard was valiantly trying to fend them off with a folding chair.

"Is that Ernest Hemingway?" Alistair asked.

"Yep. Don't let him see you, though. He'll feed you to the Mome Wraiths."

"Hemingway doesn't like me either?" Alistair asked.

"Not even a little bit," Bombo replied. "In fact, to say he dislikes you would be a fantastic understatement."

They raced across the gymnasium and headed for the locker room, because it was the only internal door in the building and the only direction that was mostly free of screeching Mome Wraiths. When they reached the door, Bombo threw it open. They were disappointed to see only lockers on the other side.

"Maybe there's another door," Alistair said. "Come on."

They darted past the lockers and through the shower area, and found another door deeper inside the locker room. It was constructed of ancient teak, narrow, and hung on antique hinges. It rested between two metal lockers and had a crystalline knob that seemed out of place in the utilitarian gym.

"Where does it go?" Alistair asked. "This *has* to be it. I mean, just look at it."

"There's only one way to find out," said Bombo. He opened the door, and the two men stepped through the blinding light, with no idea what they'd find on the other side.

TO BE CONTINUED IN LITERARY OUTLAW #8

"THERE IS NOTHING NOBLE IN BEING SUPERIOR TO YOUR FELLOW MAN; TRUE NOBILITY IS BEING SUPERIOR TO YOUR FORMER SELF."

"THE FIRST DRAFT OF ANYTHING IS SHIT."

"ALL GOOD BOOKS ARE ALIKE IN THAT THEY ARE TRUER THAN IF THEY HAD REALLY HAPPENED AND AFTER YOU ARE FINISHED READING ONE YOU WILL FEEL THAT ALL THAT HAPPENED TO YOU AND AFTERWARDS IT ALL BELONGS TO YOU: THE GOOD AND THE BAD, THE ECSTASY, THE REMORSE AND SORROW, THE PEOPLE AND THE PLACES AND HOW THE WEATHER WAS. IF YOU CAN GET SO THAT YOU CAN GIVE THAT TO PEOPLE, THEN YOU ARE A WRITER."

— ERNEST HEMINGWAY

Chapter 3. THAR SHE BLOWS!

HOW TO DESCRIBE CAPTAIN AHAB OF THE "PEQUOD"? 'SORT OF SICK' HIS MEN CALLED HIM, BUT THERE SEEMED NO SIGN OF COMMON BODILY ILLNESS ABOUT HIM — ONLY THAT WHITE IVORY LEG, FASHIONED FROM A SPERM-WHALE'S POLISHED JAWBONE...

AY! HE WAS DISMASTED OFF JAPAN BY THE TEETH OF A GREAT WHITE WHALE, BUT HE SHIPPED ANOTHER MAST WHICH SERVES HIM JUST AS WELL!

...AND, THREADING ITS WAY FROM HIS GREY HAIRS AND CONTINUING DOWN ONE SIDE OF HIS TAWNY SCORCHED FACE — A LIVID SCAR!

THE SAME WHITE WHALE BRANDED HIS CHEEK... AND ALL HE LIVES FOR IS TO TAKE VENGEANCE AGEN THE BEAST THAT DID IT TO HIM!

AHAB SPOKE RARELY, AND FEW DARED TO ADDRESS HIM. ONE MIDDLE WATCH, STUBB, THE COCKY SECOND MATE, CAME UP FROM HIS HAMMOCK BELOW AND SMILINGLY CHAFFED HIS CAPTAIN...

CAP'N, SIR— 'TIS A SMALL FAVOUR I ASK OF YOU — YOUR IVORY LEG SOUNDS UNCOMMON LOUD ON THE DECK— MIGHT I ASK YOU TO MUFFLE ITS END WITH A WAD O' COTTON, SO THAT I MAY GET SOME SLEEP.

WHAT'S THIS, HEY?

THE CAPTAIN'S VOICE ROSE ABOVE THE HOWL OF THE WIND, CONQUERED THE THOUSAND NOTES OF THE TORTURED RIGGING...
AM I A CANNON BALL, STUBB, THAT THOU WOULDS'T WAD ME? GET BELOW TO THY NIGHTLY GRAVE! WIND THYSELF IN THY TEMPORARY SHROUD! DOWN, DOG! TO THY KENNEL!

STUBB RETIRED BELOW, HASTILY... AND SHOOK HIS HEAD TO ISHMAEL...
HE'S A QUEER 'UN! HE AIN'T IN BED MORE THAN THREE HOURS OUT O' TWENTY FOUR, AND HE DON'T SLEEP THEN!
WHAT DRIVES HIM ON? WHAT KEEPS HIM ON DECK NIGHT AND DAY IN ALL WEATHERS? WHY DOES HE SCAN THE SEA SO WILDLY?

YOU'LL FIND OUT—PRAY HEAVEN YOU DON'T LIVE TO REGRET IT!

THE·REASON FOR CAPTAIN AHAB'S CONSTANT VIGIL BECAME CLEAR SOME DAYS LATER. AT THE SEVENTH BELL OF AN AFTERNOON WATCH HE ORDERED STARBUCK TO SUMMON THE SHIP'S COMPANY AFT — WHEN EVERY MAN WAS ASSEMBLED, HE CRIED OUT IN A LOUD VOICE . . .

AHAB'S STRANGE, WILD EYES SWEPT THE WATCHING FACES BEFORE HIM...
THEN LISTEN TO ME, MEN! WHOSOEVER OF YE SINGS OUT FOR A WHITE WHALE WITH A CROOKED JAW, WITH THREE HOLES PUNCTURED IN THE STARBOARD FLUKE OF HIS TWENTY-FOOT TAIL— THAT MAN SHALL HAVE THIS SIXTEEN DOLLAR GOLD PIECE— THIS SPANISH OUNCE O' BRIGHT GOLD!

WITH THOSE WORDS, AHAB NAILED THE GOLD PIECE TO THE MAST...A TOKEN AND A REWARD FOR ALL TO SEE....
IT'S A WHITE WHALE, I SAY! SKIN YOUR EYES FOR HIM, MEN—IF YOU SEE BUT A BUBBLE— SING OUT!

QUEEQUEG AND HIS TWO FELLOW HARPOONERS, THE INDIAN TASHTEGO, AND THE NEGRO DAGGOO, STOOD BY THE RAIL.
ALL THREE STARTED AS IF STRUCK BY A SUDDEN RECOLLECTION...
CAP'N AHAB! THAT WHITE WHALE MUST BE THE SAME AS SOME CALL— MOBY DICK!
—AND HE FAN-TAILS HIS FLUKES A LITTLE CURIOUS AS HE GOES DOWN—
—AND HE HAVE PLENNY GOOD MANY IRON IN HIM HIDE TOO! ALL TWISKEE LIKE UM CORKSCREWS!

THAT'S HIM! MOBY DICK, THE VERY SAME! AND HARPOONS LIE ALL TWISTED AND WRENCHED IN HIM... YE HAVE SEEN HIM INDEED! DEATH AND DEMONS, MEN! IT IS MOBY DICK YE HAVE SEEN —MOBY DICK! MOBY DICK!

AYE! AND 'TWAS MOBY DICK THAT DISMASTED ME, MADE A POOR PEGGING LUBBER O' ME FOR EVER AND A DAY! BUT I'LL CHASE HIM ROUND GOOD HOPE, ROUND THE HORN, TO THE END O' THE SEAS, BEFORE I GIVE UP! WITH YOUR HELP, MY HEARTIES, I'LL DRIVE IRON INTO HIS ACCURSED WHITE HIDE!

ROUSED BY AHAB'S WORDS AND BY THE PROMISE OF GOLD, THE CREW CHEERED HEARTILY... BUT FIRST MATE STARBUCK GROWLED SOURLY....
I CAME TO HUNT WHALES FOR OIL, CAP'N— NOT FOR VENGEANCE ON A DUMB BRUTE THAT SMOTE YOU FROM BLIND INSTINCT!
SILENCE, STARBUCK! WILL THE BEST WHALEMAN IN NANTUCKET HANG BACK WHEN EVERY FOREMAST HAND IS READY WITH HIS LIFE-BLOOD? BE SILENT — AND OBEY!

STARBUCK'S REPLY WAS SPOKEN TOO QUIETLY FOR AHAB'S EARS — BUT ISHMAEL THE SEAFARING-SCHOOLMASTER, HEARD IT— AND NEVER FORGOT IT.
THEN GOD KEEP ME — AND GOD KEEP US ALL!

SO THE "PEQUOD" SAILED ON . . . SOUTHWARDS . . . EVER SOUTHWARDS . . . INTO THE WILDERNESS OF BARREN OCEAN . . . WITH THE CRAZED WILL OF ONE MAN DRIVING HER ON !
THE HUNT WAS ON . . . AND THE QUARRY WAS THE GREAT WHITE WHALE . . . *MOBY DICK !*

IT HAPPENED TWO DAYS LATER, IN THE FORENOON WATCH... TASHTEGO WAS HIGH ALOFT IN THE CROSS. TREES... HIS VOICE DROPPED TO THE DECK!
WHALE-HO! THAR SHE BLOWS!

INSTANTLY THE THREE GREAT WHALEBOATS WERE MANNED AND SWUNG OUTBOARD... ISHMAEL, AS BOW OARSMAN IN STARBUCK'S BOAT, JOINED QUEEQUEG IN THE BOWS....
IS IT MOBY DICK, I WONDER?
MEBBE SO — WE SEE PLENTY QUICK SOON —

CAPTAIN AHAB STOMPED ON DECK BEFORE THE TACKLES BEGAN TO CREAK... AND WITH HIM CAME A STRANGE, UNEARTHLY FIGURE!
YOU WILL ACCOMPANY ME FEDALLAH!
YESSS—

THE MEN STARED, OPEN-MOUTHED, AS THE CAPTAIN'S WEIRD COMPANION TOOK HIS PLACE BY AHAB'S SIDE IN THE FIRST BOAT...
I NEVER SEEN THE LIKE O' HIM AFORE!
HE MUST HAVE COME ABOARD AT DEAD O' NIGHT ALONGER THE CAP'N — 'TIS THE FIRST TIME HE'S SET FOOT ON THE UPPER DECK THIS VOYAGE—

AS STARBUCK'S BOAT PULLED OUT FROM UNDER THE SHIP'S LEE, ISHMAEL CAUGHT A GLIMPSE OF THE TURBANED STRANGER...
HEAVEN PRESERVE US! HE'S A MANILLA! FEARED BY ALL HONEST MARINERS — 'TIS SAID THAT MANILLAS ARE AGENTS, ON THE WATER, OF THEIR LORD, THE DEVIL!
HEY! MISTER STARBUCK! WHAT MANNER OF MAN IS THAT IN THE CAPTAIN'S BOAT?

ALL THOUGHT OF STARBUCK'S STRANGE EXPLANATION WAS DASHED FROM THE MINDS OF THE MEN IN HIS BOAT... AS A MASSIVE TAIL ROSE IN A FLURRY OF FOAM AND TOWERED HIGH ABOVE THEM!
HOLD WATER STARBOARD! GIVE WAY PORT! STAND BY WITH YOUR IRON, QUEEQUEG— MAKE READY TO STRIKE!

SKILFULLY BREASTING HIS BOAT OVER THE TORTURED WASH, STARBUCK YELLED HIS NEXT ORDER...
STRIKE HOME, QUEEQUEG! STRIKE HARD AN' TRUE!

BUT A VOICE — LOUDER THAN THE FIRST MATE'S — STAYED QUEEQUEG'S ARM!
AVAST! AVAST THERE, I SAY, HEATHEN! HAST THOU BLIND BEADS INSTEAD OF EYES? THAT IS NO WHITE WHALE — THAT IS NO MOBY DICK!

THE WHALE DIVED IN A BOILING WASH — AND AHAB STEERED HIS BOAT ALONGSIDE STARBUCK'S...
YONDER WAS A WHALE — AND WE ARE WHALING MEN!
SILENCE! MOBY DICK IS OUR QUARRY, AND NO IRON SHALL BE WASTED ON ANY OTHER — BACK TO THE SHIP! SAY NO MORE!

IN MOODY SILENCE, THE BOATS WERE FINALLY HOISTED INBOARD... AND IT WAS ISHMAEL WHO VOICED THE THOUGHTS THAT RAN THROUGH ALL THEIR MINDS...
WHAT MANNER OF MAN IS HE? WHAT MANNER OF SHIP IS THIS? WE MAY SAIL THE SEVEN SEAS TILL DOOMSDAY IN SEARCH OF MOBY DICK — WITH A CRAZED CAPTAIN WHO GOES AFTER HIS QUARRY IN THE COMPANY OF A HEATHEN WITCH-DOCTOR!

THE ADVENTURES OF PENROD

BY BOOTH TARKINGTON

CHAPTER XXI
RUPE COLLINS

FOR SEVERAL DAYS AFTER THIS, PENROD thought of growing up to be a monk, and engaged in good works so far as to carry some kittens (that otherwise would have been drowned) and a pair of Margaret's outworn dancing-slippers to a poor, ungrateful old man sojourning in a shed up the alley. And although Mr. Robert Williams, after a very short interval, began to leave his guitar on the front porch again, exactly as if he thought nothing had happened, Penrod, with his younger vision of a father's mood, remained coldly distant from the Jones neighbourhood. With his own family his manner was gentle, proud and sad, but not for long enough to frighten them. The change came with mystifying abruptness at the end of the week.

It was Duke who brought it about.

Duke could chase a much bigger dog out of the Schofields' yard and far down the street. This might be thought to indicate unusual valour on the part of Duke and cowardice on that of the bigger dogs whom he undoubtedly put to rout. On the contrary, all such flights were founded in mere superstition, for dogs are even more superstitious than boys and coloured people; and the most firmly established of all dog superstitions is that any dog—be he the smallest and feeblest in the world—can whip any trespasser whatsoever.

A rat-terrier believes that on his home grounds he can whip an elephant. It follows, of course, that a big dog, away from his own home, will run from a little dog in the little dog's neighbourhood. Otherwise, the big dog must face a charge of inconsistency, and dogs are as consistent as they are superstitious. A dog believes in war, but he is convinced that there are times when it is moral to run; and the thoughtful physiognomist, seeing a big dog fleeing out of a little dog's yard, must observe that the expression of the big dog's face is more conscientious than alarmed: it is the expression of a person performing a duty to himself.

Penrod understood these matters perfectly; he knew that the gaunt brown hound Duke chased up the alley had fled only out of deference to a custom, yet Penrod could not refrain from bragging of Duke to the hound's owner, a fat-faced stranger of twelve or thirteen, who had wandered into the neighbourhood.

"You better keep that ole yellow dog o' yours back," said Penrod ominously, as he climbed the fence. "You better catch him and hold him till I get mine inside the yard again. Duke's chewed up some pretty bad bulldogs around here."

The fat-faced boy gave Penrod a fishy stare. "You'd oughta learn him not to do that," he said. "It'll make him sick."

"What will?"

The stranger laughed raspingly and gazed up the alley, where the hound, having come to a halt, now coolly sat down, and, with an expression of roguish benevolence, patronizingly watched the tempered fury of Duke, whose assaults and barkings were becoming perfunctory.

"What'll make Duke sick?" Penrod demanded.

"Eatin' dead bulldogs people leave around here."

This was not improvisation but formula, adapted from other occasions to the present encounter; nevertheless, it was new to Penrod, and he was so taken with it that resentment lost itself in admiration. Hastily committing the gem to memory for use upon a dog-owning friend, he inquired in a sociable tone:

"What's your dog's name?"

"Dan. You better call your ole pup, 'cause Dan eats LIVE dogs."

Dan's actions poorly supported his master's assertion, for, upon Duke's ceasing to bark, Dan rose and showed the most courteous interest in making the little, old dog's acquaintance. Dan had a great deal of manner, and it became plain that Duke was impressed favourably in spite of former prejudice, so that presently the two trotted amicably back to their masters and sat down with the harmonious but indifferent air of having known each other intimately for years.

They were received without comment, though both boys looked at them reflectively for a time. It was Penrod who spoke first.

"What number you go to?" (In an "oral lesson in English," Penrod had been instructed to put this question in another form: "May I ask which of our public schools you attend?")

"Me? What number do I go to?" said the stranger, contemptuously. "I don't go to NO number in vacation!"

"I mean when it ain't."

"Third," returned the fat-faced boy. "I got 'em ALL scared in THAT school."

"What of?" innocently asked Penrod, to whom "the Third"—in a distant part of town—was undiscovered country.

"What of? I guess you'd soon see what of, if you ever was in that school about one day. You'd be lucky if you got out alive!"

"Are the teachers mean?"

The other boy frowned with bitter scorn. "Teachers! Teachers don't order ME around, I can tell you! They're mighty careful how they try to run over Rupe Collins."

"Who's Rupe Collins?"

"Who is he?" echoed the fat-faced boy incredulously. "Say, ain't you got ANY sense?"

"What?"

"Say, wouldn't you be just as happy if you had SOME sense?"

"Ye-es." Penrod's answer, like the look he lifted to the impressive stranger, was meek and placative. "Rupe Collins is the principal at your school, guess."

The other yelled with jeering laughter, and mocked Penrod's manner and voice. "'Rupe Collins is the principal at your school, I guess!'" He laughed harshly again, then suddenly showed truculence. "Say, 'bo, whyn't you learn enough to go in the house when it rains? What's the matter of you, anyhow?"

"Well," urged Penrod timidly, "nobody ever TOLD me who Rupe Collins is: I got a RIGHT to think he's the principal, haven't I?"

The fat-faced boy shook his head disgustedly. "Honest, you make me sick!"

Penrod's expression became one of despair. "Well, who IS he?" he cried.

"'Who IS he?'" mocked the other, with a scorn that withered. "'Who IS he?' ME!"

"Oh!" Penrod was humiliated but relieved: he felt that he had proved himself criminally ignorant, yet a peril seemed to have passed. "Rupe Collins is your name, then, I guess. I kind of thought it was, all the time."

The fat-faced boy still appeared embittered, burlesquing this speech in a hateful falsetto. "'Rupe Collins is YOUR name, then, I guess!' Oh, you 'kind of thought it was, all the time,' did you?" Suddenly concentrating his brow into a histrionic scowl he thrust his face within an inch of Penrod's. "Yes, sonny, Rupe Collins is my name, and you better look out what you say when he's around or you'll get in big trouble! YOU UNDER-STAND THAT, 'BO?"

Penrod was cowed but fascinated: he felt that there was something dangerous and dashing about this newcomer.

"Yes," he said, feebly, drawing back. "My name's Penrod Schofield."

"Then I reckon your father and mother ain't got good sense," said Mr. Collins promptly, this also being formula.

"Why?"

"'Cause if they had they'd of give you a good name!" And the agreeable youth instantly rewarded himself for the wit with another yell of rasping laughter, after which he pointed suddenly at Penrod's right hand.

"Where'd you get that wart on your finger?" he demanded severely.

"Which finger?" asked the mystified Penrod, extending his hand.

"The middle one."

"Where?"

"There!" exclaimed Rupe Collins, seizing and vigorously twisting the wartless finger naively offered for his inspection.

"Quit!" shouted Penrod in agony. "QUEE-yut!"

"Say your prayers!" commanded Rupe, and continued to twist the luckless finger until Penrod writhed to his knees.

"OW!" The victim, released, looked grievously upon the still painful finger.

At this Rupe's scornful expression altered to one of contrition. "Well, I declare!" he exclaimed remorsefully. "I didn't s'pose it would hurt. Turn about's fair play; so now you do that to me."

He extended the middle finger of his left hand and Penrod promptly seized it, but did not twist it, for he was instantly swung round with his back to his amiable new acquaintance: Rupe's right hand operated upon the back of Penrod's slender neck; Rupe's knee tortured the small of Penrod's back.

"OW!" Penrod bent far forward involuntarily and went to his knees again.

"Lick dirt," commanded Rupe, forcing the captive's face to the sidewalk; and the suffering Penrod completed this ceremony.

Mr. Collins evinced satisfaction by means of his horse laugh.

"You'd last jest about one day up at the Third!" he said. "You'd come runnin' home, yellin' 'MOM-MUH, MOM-muh,' before recess was over!"

"No, I wouldn't," Penrod protested rather weakly, dusting his knees.

"You would, too!"

"No, I w—"

"Looky here," said the fat-faced boy, darkly, "what you mean, counterdick-ing me?"

He advanced a step and Penrod hast-ily qualified his contradiction.

"I mean, I don't THINK I would. I—"

"You better look out!" Rupe moved closer, and unexpectedly grasped the back of Penrod's neck again. "Say, 'I WOULD run home yellin' "MOM-muh!"'"

"Ow! I WOULD run home yellin' 'Mom-muh.'"

"There!" said Rupe, giving the help-less nape a final squeeze. "That's the way we do up at the Third."

Penrod rubbed his neck and asked meekly:

"Can you do that to any boy up at the Third?"

"See here now," said Rupe, in the tone of one goaded beyond all endur-ance, "YOU say if I can! You better say it quick, or—"

"I knew you could," Penrod inter-posed hastily, with the pathetic semblance of a laugh. "I only said that in fun."

"In ,fun'!" repeated Rupe stormily. "You better look out how you—"

"Well, I SAID I wasn't in earnest!" Penrod retreated a few steps. "*I* knew you could, all the time. I expect *I* could do it to some of the boys up at the Third, myself. Couldn't I?"

"No, you couldn't."

"Well, there must be SOME boy up there that I could—"

"No, they ain't! You better—"

"I expect not, then," said Penrod, quickly.

"You BETTER 'expect not.' Didn't I tell you once you'd never get back alive if you ever tried to come up around the Third? You want me to SHOW you how we do up there, 'bo?"

He began a slow and deadly advance, whereupon Penrod timidly offered a diversion:

"Say, Rupe, I got a box of rats in our stable under a glass cover, so you can watch 'em jump around when you ham-mer on the box. Come on and look at 'em."

"All right," said the fat-faced boy, slightly mollified. "We'll let Dan kill 'em."

"No, SIR! I'm goin' to keep 'em. They're kind of pets; I've had 'em all summer—I got names for em, and—"

"Looky here, 'bo. Did you hear me say we'll let 'Dan kill 'em?"

"Yes, but I won't—"

"WHAT won't you?" Rupe became sinister immediately. "It seems to me you're gettin' pretty fresh around here."

"Well, I don't want—"

Mr. Collins once more brought into play the dreadful eye-to-eye scowl as prac-tised "up at the Third," and, sometimes, also by young leading men upon the stage. Frowning appallingly, and thrust-ing forward his underlip, he placed his nose almost in contact with the nose of Penrod, whose eyes naturally became crossed.

"Dan kills the rats. See?" hissed the fat-faced boy, maintaining the horrible juxtaposition.

"Well, all right," said Penrod, swal-lowing. "I don't want 'em much." And when the pose had been relaxed, he stared at his new friend for a moment, almost with reverence. Then he brightened.

"Come on, Rupe!" he cried enthusi-astically, as he climbed the fence. "We'll give our dogs a little live meat—'bo!"

CHAPTER XXII
THE IMITATOR

At the dinner-table, that evening, Penrod Surprised his family by remark-ing, in a voice they had never heard him attempt—a law-giving voice of inten-tional gruffness:

"Any man that's makin' a hunderd dollars a month is makin' good money."

"What?" asked Mr. Schofield, star-ing, for the previous conversation had concerned the illness of an infant relative in Council Bluffs.

"Any man that's makin' a hunderd dollars a month is makin' good money."

"What IS he talking about!" Marga-ret appealed to the invisible.

"Well," said Penrod, frowning, "that's what foremen at the ladder works get."

"How in the world do you know?" asked his mother.

"Well, I KNOW it! A hunderd dollars a month is good money, I tell you!"

"Well, what of it?" said the father, impatiently.

"Nothin'. I only said it was good money."

Mr. Schofield shook his head, dismissing the subject; and here he made a mistake: he should have followed up his son's singular contribution to the conversation. That would have revealed the fact that there was a certain Rupe Collins whose father was a foreman at the ladder works. All clues are important when a boy makes his first remark in a new key.

"'Good money'?" repeated Margaret, curiously. "What is 'good' money?"

Penrod turned upon her a stern glance. "Say, wouldn't you be just as happy if you had SOME sense?"

"Penrod!" shouted his father. But Penrod's mother gazed with dismay at her son: he had never before spoken like that to his sister.

Mrs. Schofield might have been more dismayed than she was, if she had realized that it was the beginning of an epoch. After dinner, Penrod was slightly scalded in the back as the result of telling Della, the cook, that there was a wart on the middle finger of her right hand. Della thus proving poor material for his new manner to work upon, he approached Duke, in the backyard, and, bending double, seized the lowly animal by the forepaws.

"I let you know my name's Penrod Schofield," hissed the boy. He protruded his underlip ferociously, scowled, and thrust forward his head until his nose touched the dog's. "And you better look out when Penrod Schofield's around, or you'll get in big trouble! YOU UNDERSTAN' THAT, 'BO?"

The next day, and the next, the increasing change in Penrod puzzled and distressed his family, who had no idea of its source.

How might they guess that hero-worship takes such forms? They were vaguely conscious that a rather shabby boy, not of the neighbourhood, came to "play" with Penrod several times; but they failed to connect this circumstance with the peculiar behaviour of the son of the house, whose ideals (his father remarked) seemed to have suddenly become identical with those of Gyp the Blood.

Meanwhile, for Penrod himself, "life had taken on new meaning, new richness." He had become a fighting man—in conversation at least. "Do you want to know how I do when they try to slip up on me from behind?" he asked Della. And he enacted for her unappreciative eye a scene of fistic manoeuvres wherein he held an imaginary antagonist helpless in a net of stratagems.

Frequently, when he was alone, he would outwit, and pummel this same enemy, and, after a cunning feint, land a dolorous stroke full upon a face of air. "There! I guess you'll know better next time. That's the way we do up at the Third!"

Sometimes, in solitary pantomime, he encountered more than one opponent at a time, for numbers were apt to come upon him treacherously, especially at a little after his rising hour, when he might be caught at a disadvantage—perhaps standing on one leg to encase the other in his knickerbockers. Like lightning, he would hurl the trapping garment from him, and, ducking and pivoting, deal great sweeping blows among the circle of sneaking devils. (That was how he broke the clock in his bedroom.) And while these battles were occupying his attention, it was a waste of voice to call him to breakfast, though if his mother, losing patience, came to his room, she would find him seated on the bed pulling at a stocking. "Well, ain't I coming fast as I CAN?"

At the table and about the house generally he was bumptious, loud with fatuous misinformation, and assumed a domineering tone, which neither satire nor reproof seemed able to reduce: but it was among his own intimates that his new superiority was most outrageous. He twisted the fingers and squeezed the necks of all the boys of the neighbourhood, meeting their indignation with a hoarse and rasping laugh he had acquired after short practice in the stable, where he jeered and taunted the lawn-mower, the garden-scythe and the wheelbarrow quite out of countenance.

Likewise he bragged to the other boys by the hour, Rupe Collins being the chief subject of encomium—next to Penrod himself. "That's the way we do up at the Third," became staple explanation of violence, for Penrod, like Tartarin, was plastic in the hands of his own imagination, and at times convinced himself that he really was one of those dark and murderous spirits exclusively of whom "the Third" was composed—according to Rupe Collins.

Then, when Penrod had exhausted himself repeating to nausea accounts of the prowess of himself and his great friend, he would turn to two other subjects for vainglory. These were his father and Duke.

Mothers must accept the fact that between babyhood and manhood their sons do not boast of them. The boy, with boys, is a Choctaw; and either the influence or the protection of women is shameful. "Your mother won't let you," is an insult. But, "My father won't let me," is a dignified explanation and cannot be hooted. A boy is ruined among his fellows if he talks much of his mother or sisters; and he must recognize it as his duty to offer at least the appearance of persecution to all things ranked as female, such as cats and every species of fowl. But he must champion his father and his dog, and, ever, ready to pit either against any challenger, must picture both as ravening for battle and absolutely unconquerable.

Penrod, of course, had always talked by the code, but, under the new stimulus, Duke was represented virtually as a cross between Bob, Son of Battle, and a South American vampire; and this in spite of the fact that Duke himself often sat close by, a living lie, with the hope of peace in his heart. As for Penrod's father, that gladiator was painted as of sentiments and dimensions suitable to a super-demon composed of equal parts of Goliath, Jack Johnson and the Emperor Nero.

Even Penrod's walk was affected; he adopted a gait which was a kind of taunting swagger; and, when he passed other children on the street, he practised the habit of feinting a blow; then, as the victim dodged, he rasped the triumphant horse laugh which he gradually mastered to horrible perfection. He did this to Marjorie Jones—ay! this was their next meeting, and such is Eros, young! What was even worse, in Marjorie's opinion, he went on his way without explanation, and left her standing on the corner talking about it, long after he was out of hearing.

Within five days from his first encounter with Rupe Collins, Penrod had become unbearable. He even almost alienated Sam Williams, who for a time submitted to finger twisting and neck squeezing and the new style of conversation, but finally declared that Penrod made him "sick." He made the statement with fervour, one sultry afternoon, in Mr. Schofield's stable, in the presence of Herman and Verman.

"You better look out, 'bo," said Penrod, threateningly. "I'll show you a little how we do up at the Third."

"Up at the Third!" Sam repeated with scorn. "You haven't ever been up there."

"I haven't?" cried Penrod. "I HAVEN'T?"

"No, you haven't!"

"Looky here!" Penrod, darkly argumentative, prepared to perform the eye-to-eye business. "When haven't I been up there?"

"You haven't NEVER been up there!" In spite of Penrod's closely approaching nose Sam maintained his ground, and appealed for confirmation. "Has he, Herman?"

"I don' reckon so," said Herman, laughing.

"WHAT!" Penrod transferred his nose to the immediate vicinity of Herman's nose. "You don't reckon so, 'bo, don't you? You better look out how you reckon around here! YOU UNDERSTAN' THAT, 'BO?"

Herman bore the eye-to-eye very well; indeed, it seemed to please him, for he continued to laugh while Verman chuckled delightedly. The brothers had been in the country picking berries for a week, and it happened that this was their first experience of the new manifestation of Penrod.

"HAVEN'T I been up at the Third?" the sinister Penrod demanded.

"I don' reckon so. How come you ast ME?"

"Didn't you just hear me SAY I been up there?"

"Well," said Herman mischievously, "hearin' ain't believin'!"

Penrod clutched him by the back of the neck, but Herman, laughing loudly, ducked and released himself at once, retreating to the wall.

"You take that back!" Penrod shouted, striking out wildly.

"Don' git mad," begged the small darky, while a number of blows falling upon his warding arms failed to abate his amusement, and a sound one upon the cheek only made him laugh the more unrestrainedly. He behaved exactly as if Penrod were tickling him, and his brother, Verman, rolled with joy in a wheelbarrow. Penrod pummelled till he was tired, and produced no greater effect.

"There!" he panted, desisting finally. "NOW I reckon you know whether I been up there or not!"

Herman rubbed his smitten cheek. "Pow!" he exclaimed. "Pow-ee! You cert'ny did lan' me good one NAT time! Oo-ee! she HURT!"

"You'll get hurt worse'n that," Penrod assured him, "if you stay around here much. Rupe Collins is comin' this afternoon, he said. We're goin' to make some policemen's billies out of the rake handle."

"You go' spoil new rake you' pa bought?"

"What do WE care? I and Rupe got to have billies, haven't we?"

"How you make 'em?"

"Melt lead and pour in a hole we're goin' to make in the end of 'em. Then we're goin' to carry 'em in our pockets, and if anybody says anything to us—OH, oh! look out! They won't get a crack on the head—OH, no!"

"When's Rupe Collins coming?" Sam Williams inquired rather uneasily. He had heard a great deal too much of this personage, but as yet the pleasure of actual acquaintance had been denied him.

"He's liable to be here any time," answered Penrod. "You better look out. You'll be lucky if you get home alive, if you stay till HE comes."

"I ain't afraid of him," Sam returned, conventionally.

"You are, too!" (There was some truth in the retort.) "There ain't any boy in this part of town but me that wouldn't be afraid of him. You'd be afraid to talk to him. You wouldn't get a word out of your mouth before old Rupie'd have you where you'd wished you never come around HIM, lettin' on like you was so much! YOU wouldn't run home yellin' 'Mom-muh' or nothin'! OH, no!"

"Who Rupe Collins?" asked Herman.

"'Who Rupe Collins?'" Penrod mocked, and used his rasping laugh, but, instead of showing fright, Herman appeared to think he was meant to laugh, too; and so he did, echoed by Verman. "You just hang around here a little while longer," Penrod added, grimly, "and you'll find out who Rupe Collins is, and I pity YOU when you do!"

"What he go' do?"

"You'll see; that's all! You just wait and—"

At this moment a brown hound ran into the stable through the alley door, wagged a greeting to Penrod, and fraternized with Duke. The fat-faced boy appeared upon the threshold and gazed coldly about the little company in the carriage-house, whereupon the coloured brethren, ceasing from merriment, were instantly impassive, and Sam Williams moved a little nearer the door leading into the yard.

Obviously, Sam regarded the newcomer as a redoubtable if not ominous figure. He was a head taller than either Sam or Penrod; head and shoulders taller than Herman, who was short for his age; and Verman could hardly be used for purposes of comparison at all, being a mere squat brown spot, not yet quite nine years on this planet. And to Sam's mind, the aspect of Mr. Collins realized Penrod's portentous foreshadowings. Upon the fat face there was an expression of truculent intolerance which had been cultivated by careful habit to such perfection that Sam's heart sank at sight of it. A somewhat enfeebled twin to this expression had of late often decorated the visage of Penrod, and appeared upon that ingenuous surface now, as he advanced to welcome the eminent visitor.

The host swaggered toward the door with a great deal of shoulder movement, carelessly feinting a slap at Verman in passing, and creating by various means the atmosphere of a man who has contemptuously amused himself with underlings while awaiting an equal.

"Hello, ,bo!" Penrod said in the deepest voice possible to him.

"Who you callin' 'bo?" was the ungracious response, accompanied by immediate action of a similar nature. Rupe held Penrod's head in the crook of an elbow and massaged his temples with a hard-pressing knuckle.

"I was only in fun, Rupie," pleaded the sufferer, and then, being set free, "Come here, Sam," he said.

"What for?"

Penrod laughed pityingly. "Pshaw, I ain't goin' to hurt you. Come on." Sam, maintaining his position near the other door, Penrod went to him and caught him round the neck.

"Watch me, Rupie!" Penrod called, and performed upon Sam the knuckle operation which he had himself just undergone, Sam submitting mechanically, his eyes fixed with increasing uneasiness upon Rupe Collins. Sam had a premonition that something even more painful than Penrod's knuckle was going to be inflicted upon him.

"THAT don' hurt," said Penrod, pushing him away.

"Yes, it does, too!" Sam rubbed his temple.

"Puh! It didn't hurt me, did it, Rupie? Come on in, Rupe: show this baby where he's got a wart on his finger."

"You showed me that trick," Sam objected. "You already did that to me. You tried it twice this afternoon and I don't know how many times before, only you weren't strong enough after the first time. Anyway, I know what it is, and I don't—"

"Come on, Rupe," said Penrod. "Make the baby lick dirt."

At this bidding, Rupe approached, while Sam, still protesting, moved to the threshold of the outer door; but Penrod seized him by the shoulders and swung him indoors with a shout.

"Little baby wants to run home to its Mom-muh! Here he is, Rupie."

Thereupon was Penrod's treachery to an old comrade properly rewarded, for as the two struggled, Rupe caught each by the back of the neck, simultaneously, and, with creditable impartiality, forced both boys to their knees.

"Lick dirt!" he commanded, forcing them still forward, until their faces were close to the stable floor.

At this moment he received a real surprise. With a loud whack something struck the back of his head, and, turning, he beheld Verman in the act of lifting a piece of lath to strike again.

"Em moys ome!" said Verman, the Giant Killer.

"He tongue-tie'," Herman explained. "He say, let 'em boys alone."

Rupe addressed his host briefly:

"Chase them nigs out o' here!"

"Don' call me nig," said Herman. "I mine my own biznuss. You let 'em boys alone."

Rupe strode across the still prostrate Sam, stepped upon Penrod, and, equipping his countenance with the terrifying scowl and protruded jaw, lowered his head to the level of Herman's.

"Nig, you'll be lucky if you leave here alive!" And he leaned forward till his nose was within less than an inch of Herman's nose.

It could be felt that something awful was about to happen, and Penrod, as he rose from the floor, suffered an unexpected twinge of apprehension and remorse: he hoped that Rupe wouldn't REALLY hurt Herman. A sudden dislike of Rupe and Rupe's ways rose within him, as he looked at the big boy overwhelming the little darky with that ferocious scowl. Penrod, all at once, felt sorry about something indefinable; and, with equal vagueness, he felt foolish. "Come on, Rupe," he suggested, feebly, "let Herman go, and let's us make our billies out of the rake handle."

The rake handle, however, was not available, if Rupe had inclined to favour the suggestion. Verman had discarded his lath for the rake, which he was at this moment lifting in the air.

"You ole black nigger," the fat-faced boy said venomously to Herman, "I'm agoin' to—"

But he had allowed his nose to remain too long near Herman's.

Penrod's familiar nose had been as close with only a ticklish spinal effect upon the not very remote descendant of Congo man-eaters. The result produced by the glare of Rupe's unfamiliar eyes, and by the dreadfully suggestive proximity of Rupe's unfamiliar nose, was altogether different. Herman's and Verman's Bangala great-grandfathers never considered people of their own jungle neighbourhood proper material for a meal, but they looked upon strangers especially truculent strangers—as distinctly edible.

Penrod and Sam heard Rupe suddenly squawk and bellow; saw him writhe and twist and fling out his arms like flails, though without removing his face from its juxtaposition; indeed, for a moment, the two heads seemed even closer.

Then they separated—and battle was on!

CHAPTER XXIII
COLOURED TROOPS IN ACTION

How neat and pure is the task of the chronicler who has the tale to tell of a "good rousing fight" between boys or men who fight in the "good old English way," according to a model set for fights in books long before Tom Brown went to Rugby. There are seconds and rounds and rules of fair-play, and always there is great good feeling in the end—though sometimes, to vary the model, "the Butcher" defeats the hero—and the chronicler who stencils this fine old pattern on his page is certain of applause as the stirrer of "red blood." There is no surer recipe.

But when Herman and Verman set to 't the record must be no more than a few fragments left by the expurgator. It has been perhaps sufficiently suggested that the altercation in Mr. Schofield's stable opened with mayhem in respect to the aggressor's nose. Expressing vocally his indignation and the extremity of his pained surprise, Mr. Collins stepped backward, holding his left hand over his nose, and striking at Herman with his right. Then Verman hit him with the rake.

Verman struck from behind. He struck as hard as he could. And he struck with the tines down—For, in his simple, direct African way he wished to kill his enemy, and he wished to kill him as soon as possible. That was his single, earnest purpose.

On this account, Rupe Collins was peculiarly unfortunate. He was plucky and he enjoyed conflict, but neither his ambitions nor his anticipations had ever included murder. He had not learned that an habitually aggressive person runs the danger of colliding with beings in one of those lower stages of evolution wherein theories about "hitting below the belt" have not yet made their appearance.

The rake glanced from the back of Rupe's head to his shoulder, but it felled him. Both darkies jumped full upon him instantly, and the three rolled and twisted upon the stable-floor, unloosing upon the air sincere maledictions closely connected with complaints of cruel and unusual treatment; while certain expressions of feeling presently emanating from Herman and Verman indicated that Rupe Collins, in this extremity, was proving himself not too slavishly addicted to fighting by rule. Dan and Duke, mistaking all for mirth, barked gayly.

From the panting, pounding, yelling heap issued words and phrases hitherto quite unknown to Penrod and Sam; also, a hoarse repetition in the voice of Rupe concerning his ear left it not to be doubted that additional mayhem was taking place. Appalled, the two spectators retreated to the doorway nearest the yard, where they stood dumbly watching the cataclysm.

The struggle increased in primitive simplicity: time and again the howling Rupe got to his knees only to go down again as the earnest brothers, in their own way, assisted him to a more reclining position. Primal forces operated here, and the two blanched, slightly higher products of evolution, Sam and Penrod, no more thought of interfering than they would have thought of interfering with an earthquake.

At last, out of the ruck rose Verman, disfigured and maniacal. With a wild eye he looked about him for his trusty rake; but Penrod, in horror, had long since thrown the rake out into the yard. Naturally, it had not seemed necessary to remove the lawn-mower.

The frantic eye of Verman fell upon the lawn-mower, and instantly he leaped to its handle. Shrilling a wordless war-cry, he charged, propelling the whirling, deafening knives straight upon the prone legs of Rupe Collins. The lawn-mower was sincerely intended to pass longitudinally over the body of Mr. Collins from heel to head; and it was the time for a death-song. Black Valkyrie hovered in the shrieking air.

"Cut his gizzud out!" shrieked Herman, urging on the whirling knives.

They touched and lacerated the shin of Rupe, as, with the supreme agony of effort a creature in mortal peril puts forth before succumbing, he tore himself free of Herman and got upon his feet.

Herman was up as quickly. He leaped to the wall and seized the garden-scythe that hung there.

"I'm go to cut you' gizzud out," he announced definitely, "an' eat it!"

Rupe Collins had never run from anybody (except his father) in his life; he was not a coward; but the present situation was very, very unusual. He was already in a badly dismantled condition, and yet Herman and Verman seemed discontented with their work: Verman was swinging the grass-cutter about for a new charge, apparently still wishing to mow him, and Herman had made a quite plausible statement about what he intended to do with the scythe.

Rupe paused but for an extremely condensed survey of the horrible advance of the brothers, and then, uttering a blood-curdled scream of fear, ran out of the stable and up the alley at a speed he had never before attained, so that even Dan had hard work to keep within barking distance. And a 'cross-shoulder glance, at the corner, revealing Verman and Herman in pursuit, the latter waving his scythe overhead, Mr. Collins slackened not his gait, but, rather, out of great anguish, increased it; the while a rapidly developing purpose became firm in his mind—and ever after so remained—not only to refrain from visiting that neighbourhood again, but never by any chance to come within a mile of it.

From the alley door, Penrod and Sam watched the flight, and were without words. When the pursuit rounded the corner, the two looked wanly at each other, but neither spoke until the return of the brothers from the chase.

Herman and Verman came back, laughing and chuckling.

"Hiyi!" cackled Herman to Verman, as they came, "See ,at ole boy run!"

"Who-ee!" Verman shouted in ecstasy.

"Nev' did see boy run so fas'!" Herman continued, tossing the scythe into the wheelbarrow. "I bet he home in bed by viss time!"

Verman roared with delight, appearing to be wholly unconscious that the lids of his right eye were swollen shut and that his attire, not too finical before the struggle, now entitled him to unquestioned rank as a sansculotte. Herman was a similar ruin, and gave as little heed to his condition.

Penrod looked dazedly from Herman to Verman and back again. So did Sam Williams.

"Herman," said Penrod, in a weak voice, "you wouldn't HONEST of cut his gizzard out, would you?"

"Who? Me? I don' know. He mighty mean ole boy!" Herman shook his head gravely, and then, observing that Verman was again convulsed with unctuous merriment, joined laughter with his brother. "Sho'! I guess I uz dess TALKIN' whens I said 'at! Reckon he thought I meant it, f'm de way he tuck an' run. Hiyi! Reckon he thought ole Herman bad man! No, suh! I uz dess talkin', 'cause I nev' would cut NObody! I ain' tryin' git in no jail—NO, suh!"

Penrod looked at the scythe: he looked at Herman. He looked at the lawn-mower, and he looked at Verman.

Then he looked out in the yard at the rake. So did Sam Williams.

"Come on, Verman," said Herman. "We ain' go' 'at stove-wood f' supper yit."

Giggling reminiscently, the brothers disappeared leaving silence behind them in the carriage-house. Penrod and Sam retired slowly into the shadowy interior, each glancing, now and then, with a preoccupied air, at the open, empty doorway where the late afternoon sunshine was growing ruddy. At intervals one or the other scraped the floor reflectively with the side of his shoe. Finally, still without either having made any effort at conversation, they went out into the yard and stood, continuing their silence.

"Well," said Sam, at last, "I guess it's time I better be gettin' home. So long, Penrod!"

"So long, Sam," said Penrod, feebly.

With a solemn gaze he watched his friend out of sight. Then he went slowly into the house, and after an interval occupied in a unique manner, appeared in the library, holding a pair of brilliantly gleaming shoes in his hand.

Mr. Schofield, reading the evening paper, glanced frowningly over it at his offspring.

"Look, papa," said Penrod. "I found your shoes where you'd taken 'em off in your room, to put on your slippers, and they were all dusty. So I took 'em out on the back porch and gave 'em a good blacking. They shine up fine, don't they?"

"Well, I'll be d-dud-dummed!" said the startled Mr. Schofield.

Penrod was zigzagging back to normal.

TO BE CONTINUED IN LITERARY OUTLAW #8

...MONIQUE MONTAGNE IS GRACEFUL... AND LITHE-LIMBED... AND ALMOST WORSHIPPED...
...I laugh...
...SUZETTE DET ELST IS NOW FINISHED... NOW OVER... ALMOST BURIED...
...THIS IS THE TALE OF TWO WHO ARE APPARENT OPPOSITES... ONE WHO IS ON THE TOP, WHO SHORTLY WILL DIE ...AND ONE WHO IS... ALREADY... DEAD...
the laugh... of the graceful... DEAD!
DE LA ROSA.
WRITTEN BY ALAN HEWETSON
ILLUSTRATED BY DELA ROSA

...I...CANNOT ENDURE THIS... SHE SHOULD NOT BE SO ADMIRED... I AM THE ONE TO BE ADMIRED... I AM DESERVING... ...I WORKED TOO LONG...TOO HARD TO LET A YOUNG...
CHILD TAKE THE HONOR THAT IS RIGHTFULLY MINE...
...AND I WILL NOT LET HER...
...SUZETTE?... ...WHAT IS IT? IS SOMETHING WRONG?
NO... NOT ANY MORE...
...SUZETTE...

... I'LL STUFF HER IN HER TRUNK...
... WHEN THEY REALIZE SHE WON'T SHOW UP IN TIME FOR--
--THE NEXT PERFORMANCE THEY'LL NEED A SUBSTITUTE... AND I AM THE ONLY DANCER ABLE TO FILL HER SLIPPERS...
...YES... YES... DO YOU WANT TO DO IT SUZETTE?... I KNOW... IT'S NOT VERY KIND TO ASK YOU KNOWING HOW... HOW YOU FEEL BUT... I HAVE NO CHOICE SUZETTE... ...IT WILL JUST BE FOR ONE PERFOR-MANCE... JUST TILL WE FIND MONIQUE...
...THEY LOVE ME... ...THEY LOVE ME SO... ...LISTEN TO THEM MOAN AND MURMUR IN DELIGHT... ...I MUST BE MORE GRACEFUL THAN I WAS IN MY YOUTH... THEY WERE NOT SO APPRECIATIVE THEN...
SUZETTE... ...SUZETTE HAVE YOU SEEN MONIQUE? MY GOD THERE IS ONLY A FEW MINUTES BEFO-RE OUR SECOND PERFORMANCE AND I CAN'T FIND HER... ...NO-ONE CAN FIND HER...
...YOU'LL NEED A REPLACE-MENT...
...IT WILL BE MY PLEASURE M. TOULAC...

...BUT SHE'S DEAD... MY GOD SHE'S DEAD... SHE'S DEAD... ...I KILL HER... ...SHE'S DEAD...
MONIQUE!
...LISTEN TO THEM APPLAUD... ...NOT ME... HER... ...A DEAD CORPSE... ...THEY'RE APPLAUDING A... CORPSE...
MONIQUE... MONIQUE... WAIT... ...WAIT I WANT TO SPEAK TO YOU...
...I WANT TO FIND OUT HOW YOU ARE ALIVE WHEN I KILLED YOU...
...WHERE ARE YOU?... ...HER ROOM IS EMPTY... ...WHERE IS SHE?...
EXIT

...SHE *MUST* BE IN THE *TRUNK*...
...SHE *MUST* BE IN THE *TRUNK*... I *PUT* HER IN THE *TRUNK*... ...I *KILLED* HER... I STUFFED HER INTO THE TRUNK AFTER I SHOVED A *KNIFE* INTO HER *STOMACH*...
...IN... THE *TRUNK?*... ...MAYBE THIS IS ALL IN MY *MIND*... ...MAYBE I'M GOING *INSANE*... ...MAYBE NONE OF IT *HAPPENED*... ...MAYBE IT WAS A *NIGHTMARE* OR... OR MAYBE IT'S ONLY MY *CONSCIENCE* DRIVING ME *MAD*...
...OH LORD...
...SILLY OLD FOOL...
...HOW?... ...I... DON'T *UNDERSTAND*... I... I *KILLED* YOU...
...NO... YOU THRUST A KNIFE INTO MY STOMACH... AND... IT *AMUSED* ME TO PLAY DEAD... BUT YOU CANNOT KILL ONE WHO IS...
ALREADY DEAD SUZETTE ...AND... YOU WERE REALLY *SO FUNNY* YOU KNOW... ...STUFFING ME IN MY OWN *COFFIN-BED*...
...AND MONIQUE MONTAGNE... THE WORSHIPPED... THE LITHE-LIMBED... AND ABOVE ALL, THE GRACEFUL TOAST OF THE BALLET-CIRCUIT LAUGHED THE LAUGH OF THE GRACEFUL DEAD...

AND ALL THE GIRLS WERE NUDE

BY RICHARD MAGRUDER

APPEARANCES OFTENTIMES CAN BE deceiving, and things most certainly *aren't* always as they seem. Take the case of Nathanial Evergood, for instance.

The nature of this old man was such that nobody ever called him Nat, not even his closest working companions in the company's bookkeeping department. As long as any of them had ever known Nathanial Evergood there had never been the slightest indication of any desire of his for intimacy or even friendship.

Not once had he shared a drink or lunch or relaxed conversation with anyone, so far as his associates knew. To say Nathanial was reserved is putting it mildly.

It would be more accurate to describe this little old man as dull—completely and absolutely dull. In his appearance, his dress, his speech, in every way imaginable.

But, in addition to being quite dull—as everyone knew, Nathanial Evergood was also a thoroughly evil and obscene old man, as no one knew.

Likely, the main reason no one had ever seen the inside of Nathanial's rooms was the fear within him that his evilness and obscenity might be discovered. For Nathanial Evergood might be called a connoisseur, to slightly distort the meaning of that word. He could be called a connoisseur of femininity—from afar, and in secret, of course. An arbiter of the well-turned thigh, the rounded, dimpled bottom, the tight waist, and the high, firm bosom.

Oh, Nathanial Evergood was a connoisseur, all right. At the investigation he ventured a very rough but conservative guess that he had collected at least fifty thousand pictures of girls, in whole or in part, horizontal or vertical, semi-nude or nude, over the years.

Upon entering his living room (if that were possible), the first thing a casual observer would have noted would be the point of saturation reached by his walls in their photographic content. There were photographs of blonds and brunettes and redheads. There were pictures of thin girls, fat girls, girls with ample bosoms and girls lacking, girls holding telephones, books and ice cream cones, girls sixteen, girls twenty-five, and girls no longer girls.

There were shots in glorious color by the hundreds, originals and prints alike. But, there wasn't among them one single view of the Grand Canyon. Nor even a solitary Indian astride a tired horse, looking pensively out over the prairie. There *was* a red-skinned maiden, mind you, but she wasn't sitting a horse, and she certainly wasn't staring laconically out over any prairie, either. Rather, she appeared to be testing with her toe the water temperature of a tree-shaded brook somewhere, and she was clad in a lone, strategically-located feather.

On the tea table, in the bookshelves, in the magazine rack, and all through his rooms, one might find other evidence of this evil and obscene old man's preoccupation with womankind. But the kind of woman he was preoccupied with often wasn't the kind that married dear old dad. He subscribed to every girlie publication in the country and to several in France.

★ ★ ★

SO YOU SEE, NATHANIAL EVERGOOD WAS not only a connoisseur, he was also an avid collector. There were books and there were magazines, and there was even a deck of playing cards backed with the most astounding set of pictures you ever saw. That anyone could sit down to a game of Old Maid or Snap with *that* deck of cards is inconceivable, to say the least. But such an evil and obscene old man as Nathanial Evergood likely never played games with his cards, anyway. He would much prefer to just sit and look at them; the reverse side, of course.

He later said he probably spent almost half his really quite meager earnings for up-to-date additions to his extensive collection. The girlie magazines, playing cards and prints he received from various mail order houses, sent, as the advertisements testified, "in a plain, unmarked envelope".

But the other half of his collection—the photographs, mounted, unmounted, matte and glossy enlargements and contact prints—Nathanial Evergood came by in an entirely different—and somewhat novel—manner. These resulted from his ability as a fairly advanced amateur photographer. Over the years, Nathanial had acquired three fine cameras, an excellent enlarger, two contact printers, electronic flash units, interchangeable lenses, filters, sun shades and lens caps, extension tubes and tripods. In short, Nathanial Evergood was well-equipped to take photographs of just about everything.

He had the equipment, and he had the necessary technical knowledge and facility. But, invariably, he passed up the usual pictorial, architectural, human interest, interpretive and abstract photographs, even when the opportunities for truly fine shots were there. Instead, he took roll after roll, pack after pack and cartridge upon cartridge of girls. *Nothing* but girls. All *sorts* of girls. *Just girls!*

At the investigation Nathanial suggested that the presence of a camera, introduced on the scene in a gentlemanly and courteous manner, was enough to cause almost frenzied unlocking and unzipping by even the most demure and prudish female. "Ladies," Nathanial said wisely, "love to have their bodies recorded for posterity."

Oh, he was certainly a very evil and highly obscene old man—was Nathanial Evergood—if ever you saw one.

But the full import of what his evil old soul and obscene little mind contained would probably escape the casual observer, unless he happened onto a tiny cubbyhole at the back of the rooms occupied by Nathanial. This was the sanctum sanctorum, so to speak, of his thin little heart, for here Nathanial Evergood guarded jealously a secret utterly beyond belief.

He fancied himself to be something of an inventor. And he was, too—of a sort. His ardent and relentless pursuit of photographic subject matter during the years had led him into situations demanding full knowledge of his craft, from a technical rather than from an artistic point of view. Thus, this inventive turn of mind was given an able assist by his understanding of the theory, optics and chemistry of photography.

And now, he was just putting the finishing touches to the most important project in his entire life.

Basing his plan of action on the simple optical theory of astigmatism, Nathanial designed a lens. Astigmatism, he had learned, results in the human eye, as well as in manufactured lenses of certain formulae, in the failure of horizontal and vertical target lines to reach a common focus. So his lens was designed intentionally astigmatic, allowing focus to be brought on one group of target lines or another, but never on both simultaneously.

To the front of the lens mount he added a front-surfaced prism and a filter, carefully ground and tinted internally the precise color complement of human flesh. He reasoned, quite accurately as it turned out, that the prism would gather all the colors of light together and converge them at the focal plane of the lens as pure white, thus eliminating all color. But, at the same instant, the complement filter replaced last the flesh color of the object focused upon, and subsequently recorded on film.

Then, in one fell swoop, the lens allowed Nathanial to focus carefully on one group of target lines (in his case, the female form underneath its covering), automatically throwing an opposing group of lines out of focus (the covering over the female body, in his case). The prism was busily gathering together all color and converting it into pure white light, while lastly, the complementary filter replaced the color of flesh to the image, and finally to the photograph. You see the possibilities, of course. By replacing the normal lens of one fine camera with his invention, Nathanial Evergood was now equipped to photograph in rich, natural color the female form-divine, unfettered by any or all clothing.

★ ★ ★

WELL, THIS DAY IN PARTICULAR, NATHAnial Evergood stationed himself, poised like a pointer, at his window, camera in hand, invention in place, waiting impatiently for the first likely subject to appear. And, shameful as it must seem, this evil and obscene old man was quite noticeably drooling, right from one side of his pinched little mouth.

He heard the saucy click of her heels on the pavement a full thirty seconds before she swung gracefully into his myopic line of sight. She was blondish. Not *too* blond, understand, but just blond enough. And she was a true-blue blond at heart, if you know what I mean.

Shutter: set, at 1/200 of a second; diaphragm: f/5.6; film; Real-lifecolor; rangefinder: superimposed. Click. Click, click, click! Four shots, four beautiful pictures, in color, too, before she was gone on down the street.

With incredible speed this evil and obscene old man descended from his window perch and scuttered back to his little cubby hole. He darkened the room and unloaded the automatic sheet film holder. No attempt can be made to describe the gnawing impatience that Nathanial Evergood felt as he sloshed the sensitized emulsions through the series of solutions for the precise time required for true color rendition, as, after ninety long minutes, he washed the sheets, and finally held them up to the light for a first wide-eyed look.

She was there, alright, his swaying blond. She was there. *All* of her!

Well sir, after filling his eyes—and his evil little mind—with the four lovely images of the girl, Nathanial Evergood rushed to the downtown camera shop, and wrote out a large check for their entire supply of Real-lifecolor film. Then, back on the street, madly clicking, clicking, clicking. Every pretty girl that came along. *Every* single one!

★ ★ ★

OH, HE HAD A TIME FOR HIMSELF, DID this evil, obscene old man.

The next day was Sunday, happily for his designing brain, and there was no work. After a full night in his cubby hole developing sheet after sheet of color film, Nathanial went to the beach and, as you must know by now, set his camera shutter clicking like a miniature machine gun.

And, again, the results were spectacular, to put it mildly. The collection grew and grew and grew, and Nathanial Evergood was never wearier, or never happier. What an evil, obscene man he was!

Now, if Nathanial had stuck to his camera and to his wonderful invention, this story might never have been written. But, evil and obscene as he was, he soon began to dream of new worlds to conquer.

Simple as it had been to apply the principle of astigmatism to photography—and with such marvelous results—why not apply this same principle to his eyeglasses? This would eliminate the annoying delay of taking pictures, then developing and viewing them. To say nothing of the terrific expense involved.

Usually, when writers say, "No sooner said than done", it is often a gross exaggeration. But Nathanial *was* quick about it, nevertheless.

In short order, the problems of focus, image distortion and aberrations were ironed out, and Nathanial ventured once again out into the street to give his newest brain-child its dry-run, so to speak.

The glasses worked all right. They worked just fine. And Nathanial

Evergood, in a leering ecstasy, raced up and down the streets, peering with his watery and overworked eyes this way and that, up and down, all around and back again. For the next day or so Nathanial was busy as a bee attending every beauty contest and fashion show in town, and even found time for a quick run out to the girl's school.

THE THIRD DAY FOLLOWING THE INITIAL tests of his new seeing-eye glasses, Nathanial suddenly observed there were an uncommon lot of nicely constructed young ladies right in his own department at the office. An opportunist, if ever there was one, Nathanial thought it just might be fun to give the remarkable spectacles a chance to separate the women from the girls, and the girls from the children.

This he did and although his work suffered, he spent the better part of the day classifying the office help in various categories, and learning there were at least two ladies who fell in no classification whatsoever. It was the nicest day he had spent at the office in quite some time, he decided.

Not long after that the strain brought on by the frequent changes from his normal reading glasses to the prism spectacles became so intense that he decided there was really no good reason why he shouldn't just wear them—the new ones, of course—all the time. The better to preserve his vision, and the better to pursue his avocation.

So, he did.

And therein lay the downfall of Nathanial Evergood.

For, you see, the climax of our story comes a month later, on a sunny July day, when Nathanial made his decision to take a short stroll among the mid-day lady shoppers downtown.

Understand, with those glasses of his, Nathanial had become so accustomed to seeing his fellow creatures *au natural*, as it were, that it was on the verge of becoming almost commonplace. But, evil and obscene as he was, it was still highly diverting yet.

At any rate, on this particular day, Nathanial had made his way no more than a couple of hundred feet from his front door when a heavy hand was clamped on his shoulder and a rough voice growled, "Where you think *you're* going, you scrawny old buzzard? You oughta know better."

Nathanial Evergood spun about, suddenly petrified. The uniform, of course, was invisible, and the man was no raving beauty, he'd have said. But there was no mistaking the ugly gun and the shiny badge and the authoritative tone of voice.

"I *beg* your pardon," Nathanial spluttered indignantly. "Just what is the meaning of this ridiculous outrage?"

The beefy Irish cop was even more indignant, though. "Now, just look at yourself. I've seen absent-minded old timers parading down the street with no shoes on, or even no pants on. But just look at yourself; not a *stitch* on!"

Nathanial Evergood looked down at himself in sudden horrified realization, and looked back up as quickly. "But ... but," he began, "everybody else...." But then, of course, he had to stop.

Well, the upshot of it all was that the officer hauled him back into his rooms to get some clothes on before carting him down to the station house. As it was before they entered the apartment, Nathanial stood to get ten days probation or a token fine for forgetting all his clothes, Irish cops being ordinarily an understanding lot.

But, when confronted by the staggering array of unclad femininity, this Irishman flushed a deep red, spewed an amazed Irish blasphemy, and then roared like a lion.

And don't think the officer didn't check the evidence carefully—with the proper degree of loathing, of course—before shoving Nathanial unceremoniously down the street to call the paddy wagon. Of a certainty, things went much worse for the evil, obscene Nathanial Evergood than they might have, had not this righteously outraged policeman done his duty as he saw it.

★ ★ ★

MATTER OF FACT, THEY THREW THE BOOK at the old boy. But not until a thorough investigation was made, and not until several hundred outraged members of every morals, anti-delinquency and anti-vice committee in town had carefully checked and gasped over all the collected evidence. Never in the history of the city had there been such a hue and a cry aroused for the punishment of an offender.

So, Nathanial Evergood—evil and obscene as ever—got five years for possession of pornography, indecent exposure and other charges. In the words of the presiding jurist at the climax of the spectacular trial, "Such a sentence is far too lenient a punishment for a crime of such enormity."

And, to this very day, there rests in the files of the local constabulary, the voluminous collection of Nathanial Evergood, occupying fourteen huge, well-worn cabinets, and always on display for the indignant and affronted eyes of any anti-sin committeeman who wishes to examine it.

Also taken as evidence was Nathanial's wonderful prismatic lens and his marvelous glasses. Anytime you're by the station house, drop into the chief's office and, there in the open cabinet opposite his desk, you can see the venal objects. Now though, the lenses are pretty scratched and worn, but they're still the same two inventions of that ingenious, but evil and obscene old man, Nathanial Evergood, No. 5-049,870.

And not that it makes much difference since the case is long past and closed, but it might be interesting to point out that the chief is often seen at beauty contests and fashion shows, wearing thick-lensed glasses, which, he explains, the optometrist prescribed for his failing sight. And I don't know if it's true or not, but they say the chief is also the biggest customer the local camera shops have for a certain product called Real-lifecolor film.

Not that it makes much difference now. Nathanial Evergood is serving his sentence out, evil and obscene as ever, and the case is long past and closed.

THE END

Professional creator 40+ years
SEGA CHAKAN Video Game
CHAKAN GRAPHIC NOVELS
DRAGON WAR game system
"EVERYMAN" visual poetry
SUPERFREEK superhero spoofs
RAM Robot & Monster toys
WILDLIFE, FANTASY, BOOKS
and MUCH, MUCH, MORE!!!
www.rakgraphics.com

...THERE ARE MANY KINDS OF CORRUPT, DEGENERATE DEAD PLACES ON THIS EARTH... THE MOST TRADITIONAL THAT WE KNOW OF IN THESE AMERICAS IS THE GHOST TOWN ...THE REMNANTS OF A ONCE-PROSPEROUS SOCIETY THAT FELL APART WHEN PROGRESS CAME ALONG...
...INHABITED, THESE DAYS, BY A GHOST CORPSE WHO REFUSED TO STAY IN HIS GRAVE...
...THIS IS THE WEIRD WAY IT WAS...
THE TOWN THAT CRUMBLED
...THERE WAS ANOTHER PLACE ONCE THAT CRUMBLED... THE PLACE NAMED ATLANTIS...
...A PLACE WHERE THE EARTH ONCE HEAVED AND TWISTED IN THE PHENOMENA KNOWN AS EARTHQUAKE AND A PORTION OF THE EARTH'S CRUST SUNK BENEATH THE DEPTHS OF THE OCEANS...
...INHABITED, THESE DAYS, LIKE THE COMMON AMERICAN GHOST TOWN, BY A THING WHO REFUSED TO DIE...
...BY A THING DEGENERATED BY THE OCEANS...HALF-EATEN BY THE BEASTS OF THE SEAS... BUT STILL CLINGING TO LIFE...
REFUSING TO DIE...REFUSING TO CRUMBLE WITH THE TOWN IN WHICH IT LIVES OR... UN-LIVES...

WATCHBIRD
BY ROBERT SHECKLEY

Strange how often the Millennium has been at hand. The idea is peace on Earth, see, and the way to do it is by figuring out angles.

WHEN GELSEN ENTERED, HE SAW THAT the rest of the watchbird manufacturers were already present. There were six of them, not counting himself, and the room was blue with expensive cigar smoke.

"Hi, Charlie," one of them called as he came in.

The rest broke off conversation long enough to wave a casual greeting at him. As a watchbird manufacturer, he was a member manufacturer of salvation, he reminded himself wryly. Very exclusive. You must have a certified government contract if you want to save the human race.

"The government representative isn't here yet," one of the men told him. "He's due any minute."

"We're getting the green light," another said.

"Fine." Gelsen found a chair near the door and looked around the room. It was like a convention, or a Boy Scout rally. The six men made up for their lack of numbers by sheer volume. The president of Southern Consolidated was talking at the top of his lungs about watchbird's enormous durability. The two presidents he was talking at were grinning, nodding, one trying to interrupt with the results of a test he had run on watchbird's resourcefulness, the other talking about the new recharging apparatus.

The other three men were in their own little group, delivering what sounded like a panegyric to watchbird.

Gelsen noticed that all of them stood straight and tall, like the saviors they felt they were. He didn't find it funny. Up to a few days ago he had felt that way himself. He had considered himself a pot-bellied, slightly balding saint.

HE SIGHED AND LIGHTED A CIGARETTE. At the beginning of the project, he had been as enthusiastic as the others. He remembered saying to Macintyre, his chief engineer, "Mac, a new day is coming. Watchbird is the Answer." And Macintyre had nodded very profoundly—another watchbird convert.

How wonderful it had seemed then! A simple, reliable answer to one of mankind's greatest problems, all wrapped and packaged in a pound of incorruptible metal, crystal and plastics.

Perhaps that was the very reason he was doubting it now. Gelsen suspected that you don't solve human problems so easily. There had to be a catch somewhere.

After all, murder was an old problem, and watchbird too new a solution.

„Gentlemen—" They had been talking so heatedly that they hadn't noticed the government representative entering. Now the room became quiet at once.

"Gentlemen," the plump government man said, "the President, with the consent of Congress, has acted to form a watchbird division for every city and town in the country."

The men burst into a spontaneous shout of triumph. They were going to have their chance to save the world after all, Gelsen thought, and worriedly asked himself what was wrong with that.

He listened carefully as the government man outlined the distribution scheme. The country was to be divided into seven areas, each to be supplied and serviced by one manufacturer. This meant monopoly, of course, but a necessary one. Like the telephone service, it was in the public's best interests. You couldn't have competition in watchbird service. Watchbird was for everyone.

"The President hopes," the representative continued, "that full watchbird service will be installed in the shortest possible time. You will have top priorities on strategic metals, manpower, and so forth."

"Speaking for myself," the president of Southern Consolidated said, "I expect to have the first batch of watchbirds distributed within the week. Production is all set up."

THE REST OF THE MEN WERE EQUALLY ready. The factories had been prepared to roll out the watchbirds for months now. The final standardized equipment had been agreed upon, and only the Presidential go-ahead had been lacking.

"Fine," the representative said. "If that is all, I think we can—is there a question?"

"Yes, sir," Gelsen said. "I want to know if the present model is the one we are going to manufacture."

"Of course," the representative said. "It's the most advanced."

"I have an objection." Gelsen stood up. His colleagues were glaring coldly at him. Obviously he was delaying the advent of the golden age.

"What is your objection?" the representative asked.

"First, let me say that I am one hundred per cent in favor of a machine to stop murder. It's been needed for a long time. I object only to the watchbird's learning circuits. They serve, in effect, to animate the machine and give it a pseudo-consciousness. I can't approve of that."

"But, Mr. Gelsen, you yourself testified that the watchbird would not be completely efficient unless such circuits were introduced. Without them, the watchbirds could stop only an estimated seventy per cent of murders."

"I know that," Gelsen said, feeling extremely uncomfortable. "I believe there might be a moral danger in allowing a machine to make decisions that are rightfully Man's," he declared doggedly.

"Oh, come now, Gelsen," one of the corporation presidents said. "It's nothing of the sort. The watchbird will only reinforce the decisions made by honest men from the beginning of time."

"I think that is true," the representative agreed. "But I can understand how Mr. Gelsen feels. It is sad that we must put a human problem into the hands of a machine, sadder still that we must have a machine enforce our laws. But I ask you to remember, Mr. Gelsen, that there is no other possible way of stopping a murderer *before he strikes*. It would be unfair to the many innocent people killed every year if we were to restrict watchbird on philosophical grounds. Don't you agree that I'm right?"

"Yes, I suppose I do," Gelsen said unhappily. He had told himself all that a thousand times, but something still bothered him. Perhaps he would talk it over with Macintyre.

As the conference broke up, a thought struck him. He grinned.

A lot of policemen were going to be out of work!

"Now what do you think of that?" Officer Celtrics demanded. "Fifteen years in Homicide and a machine is replacing me." He wiped a large red hand across his forehead and leaned against the captain's desk. "Ain't science marvelous?"

Two other policemen, late of Homicide, nodded glumly.

"Don't worry about it," the captain said. "We'll find a home for you in Larceny, Celtrics. You'll like it here."

"I just can't get over it," Celtrics complained. "A lousy little piece of tin and glass is going to solve all the crimes."

"Not quite," the captain said. "The watchbirds are supposed to prevent the crimes before they happen."

"Then how'll they be crimes?" one of the policeman asked. "I mean they can't hang you for murder until you commit one, can they?"

"That's not the idea," the captain said. "The watchbirds are supposed to stop a man before he commits a murder."

"Then no one arrests him?" Celtrics asked.

"I don't know how they're going to work that out," the captain admitted.

The men were silent for a while. The captain yawned and examined his watch.

"The thing I don't understand," Celtrics said, still leaning on the captain's desk, "is just how do they do it? How did it start, Captain?"

THE CAPTAIN STUDIED CELTRICS' FACE for possible irony; after all, watchbird had been in the papers for months. But then he remembered that Celtrics, like his sidekicks, rarely bothered to turn past the sports pages.

"Well," the captain said, trying to remember what he had read in the Sunday supplements, "these scientists were working on criminology. They were studying murderers, to find out what made them tick. So they found that murderers throw out a different sort of brain wave from ordinary people. And their glands act funny, too. All this happens when they're about to commit a murder. So these scientists worked out a special machine to flash red or something when these brain waves turned on."

"Scientists," Celtrics said bitterly.

"Well, after the scientists had this machine, they didn't know what to do with it. It was too big to move around, and murderers didn't drop in often enough to make it flash. So they built it into a smaller unit and tried it out in a few police stations. I think they tried one upstate. But it didn't work so good. You couldn't get to the crime in time. That's why they built the watchbirds."

"I don't think they'll stop no criminals," one of the policemen insisted.

"They sure will. I read the test results. They can smell him out before he commits a crime. And when they reach him, they give him a powerful shock or something. It'll stop him."

"You closing up Homicide, Captain?" Celtrics asked.

"Nope," the captain said. "I'm leaving a skeleton crew in until we see how these birds do."

"Hah," Celtrics said. "Skeleton crew. That's funny."

"Sure," the captain said. "Anyhow, I'm going to leave some men on. It seems the birds don't stop all murders."

"Why not?"

"Some murderers don't have these brain waves," the captain answered, trying to remember what the newspaper article had said. "Or their glands don't work or something."

"Which ones don't they stop?" Celtrics asked, with professional curiosity.

"I don't know. But I hear they got the damned things fixed so they're going to stop all of them soon."

"How they working that?"

"They learn. The watchbirds, I mean. Just like people."

"You kidding me?"

"Nope."

"Well," Celtrics said, "I think I'll just keep old Betsy oiled, just in case. You can't trust these scientists."

"Right."

"Birds!" Celtrics scoffed.

OVER THE TOWN, THE WATCHBIRD SOARED in a long, lazy curve. Its aluminum hide glistened in the morning sun, and dots of light danced on its stiff wings. Silently it flew.

Silently, but with all senses functioning. Built-in kinesthetics told the watchbird where it was, and held it in a long search curve. Its eyes and ears operated as one unit, searching, seeking.

And then something happened! The watchbird's electronically fast reflexes picked up the edge of a sensation. A correlation center tested it, matching it with electrical and chemical data in its memory files. A relay tripped.

Down the watchbird spiraled, coming in on the increasingly strong sensation. It *smelled* the outpouring of certain glands, *tasted* a deviant brain wave.

Fully alerted and armed, it spun and banked in the bright morning sunlight.

Dinelli was so intent he didn't see the watchbird coming. He had his gun poised, and his eyes pleaded with the big grocer.

"Don't come no closer."

"You lousy little punk," the grocer said, and took another step forward. "Rob me? I'll break every bone in your puny body."

The grocer, too stupid or too courageous to understand the threat of the gun, advanced on the little thief.

"All right," Dinelli said, in a thorough state of panic. "All right, sucker, take—»

A bolt of electricity knocked him on his back. The gun went off, smashing a breakfast food display.

"What in hell?" the grocer asked, staring at the stunned thief. And then he saw a flash of silver wings. "Well, I'm really damned. Those watchbirds work!"

He stared until the wings disappeared in the sky. Then he telephoned the police.

The watchbird returned to his search curve. His thinking center correlated the new facts he had learned about murder. Several of these he hadn't known before.

This new information was simultaneously flashed to all the other watchbirds and their information was flashed back to him.

New information, methods, definitions were constantly passing between them.

Now that the watchbirds were rolling off the assembly line in a steady stream, Gelsen allowed himself to relax. A loud contented hum filled his plant. Orders were being filled on time, with top priorities given to the biggest cities in his area, and working down to the smallest towns.

"All smooth, Chief," Macintyre said, coming in the door. He had just completed a routine inspection.

"Fine. Have a seat."

The big engineer sat down and lighted a cigarette.

"We've been working on this for some time," Gelsen said, when he couldn't think of anything else.

"We sure have," Macintyre agreed. He leaned back and inhaled deeply. He had been one of the consulting engineers on the original watchbird. That was six years back. He had been working

for Gelsen ever since, and the men had become good friends.

"The thing I wanted to ask you was this—" Gelsen paused. He couldn't think how to phrase what he wanted. Instead he asked, "What do you think of the watchbirds, Mac?"

"Who, me?" The engineer grinned nervously. He had been eating, drinking and sleeping watchbird ever since its inception. He had never found it necessary to have an attitude. "Why, I think it's great."

"I don't mean that," Gelsen said. He realized that what he wanted was to have someone understand his point of view. "I mean do you figure there might be some danger in machine thinking?"

"I don't think so, Chief. Why do you ask?"

"Look, I'm no scientist or engineer. I've just handled cost and production and let you boys worry about how. But as a layman, watchbird is starting to frighten me."

"No reason for that."

"I don't like the idea of the learning circuits."

"But why not?" Then Macintyre grinned again. "I know. You're like a lot of people, Chief—afraid your machines are going to wake up and say, 'What are we doing here? Let's go out and rule the world.' Is that it?"

"Maybe something like that," Gelsen admitted.

"No chance of it," Macintyre said. "The watchbirds are complex, I'll admit, but an M.I.T. calculator is a whole lot more complex. And it hasn't got consciousness."

"No. But the watchbirds can *learn*.»

"Sure. So can all the new calculators. Do you think they'll team up with the watchbirds?"

★ ★ ★

GELSEN FELT ANNOYED AT MACINTYRE, and even more annoyed at himself for being ridiculous. "It's a fact that the watchbirds can put their learning into action. No one is monitoring them."

"So that's the trouble," Macintyre said.

"I've been thinking of getting out of watchbird." Gelsen hadn't realized it until that moment.

"Look, Chief," Macintyre said. "Will you take an engineer's word on this?"

"Let's hear it."

"The watchbirds are no more dangerous than an automobile, an IBM calculator or a thermometer. They have no more consciousness or volition than those things. The watchbirds are built to respond to certain stimuli, and to carry out certain operations when they receive that stimuli."

"And the learning circuits?"

"You have to have those," Macintyre said patiently, as though explaining the whole thing to a ten-year-old. "The purpose of the watchbird is to frustrate all murder-attempts, right? Well, only certain murderers give out these stimuli. In order to stop all of them, the watchbird has to search out new definitions of murder and correlate them with what it already knows."

"I think it's inhuman," Gelsen said.

"That's the best thing about it. The watchbirds are unemotional. Their reasoning is non-anthropomorphic. You can't bribe them or drug them. You shouldn't fear them, either."

The intercom on Gelsen's desk buzzed. He ignored it.

"I know all this," Gelsen said. "But, still, sometimes I feel like the man who invented dynamite. He thought it would only be used for blowing up tree stumps."

«*You* didn't invent watchbird."

"I still feel morally responsible because I manufacture them."

The intercom buzzed again, and Gelsen irritably punched a button.

"The reports are in on the first week of watchbird operation," his secretary told him.

"How do they look?"

„Wonderful, sir."

"Send them in in fifteen minutes." Gelsen switched the intercom off and turned back to Macintyre, who was cleaning his fingernails with a wooden match. "Don't you think that this represents a trend in human thinking? The mechanical god? The electronic father?"

"Chief," Macintyre said, "I think you should study watchbird more closely. Do you know what's built into the circuits?"

"Only generally."

"First, there is a purpose. Which is to stop living organisms from committing murder. Two, murder may be defined as an act of violence, consisting of breaking, mangling, maltreating or otherwise stopping the functions of a living organism by a living organism. Three, most murderers are detectable by certain chemical and electrical changes."

Macintyre paused to light another cigarette. "Those conditions take care of the routine functions. Then, for the learning circuits, there are two more conditions. Four, there are some living organisms who commit murder without the signs mentioned in three. Five, these can be detected by data applicable to condition two."

"I see," Gelsen said.

"You realize how foolproof it is?"

"I suppose so." Gelsen hesitated a moment. "I guess that's all."

"Right," the engineer said, and left.

Gelsen thought for a few moments. There *couldn't* be anything wrong with the watchbirds.

"Send in the reports," he said into the intercom.

HIGH ABOVE THE LIGHTED BUILDINGS OF the city, the watchbird soared. It was dark, but in the distance the watchbird could see another, and another beyond that. For this was a large city.

To prevent murder ...

There was more to watch for now. New information had crossed the invisible network that connected all watchbirds. New data, new ways of detecting the violence of murder.

There! The edge of a sensation! Two watchbirds dipped simultaneously. One had received the scent a fraction of a second before the other. He continued down while the other resumed monitoring.

Condition four, there are some living organisms who commit murder without the signs mentioned in condition three.

Through his new information, the watchbird knew by extrapolation that this organism was bent on murder, even though the characteristic chemical and electrical smells were absent.

The watchbird, all senses acute, closed in on the organism. He found what he wanted, and dived.

Roger Greco leaned against a building, his hands in his pockets. In his left hand was the cool butt of a .45. Greco waited patiently.

He wasn't thinking of anything in particular, just relaxing against a building, waiting for a man. Greco didn't know why the man was to be killed. He didn't care. Greco's lack of curiosity was part of his value. The other part was his skill.

One bullet, neatly placed in the head of a man he didn't know. It didn't excite him or sicken him. It was a job, just like anything else. You killed a man. So?

As Greco's victim stepped out of a building, Greco lifted the .45 out of his pocket. He released the safety and braced the gun with his right hand. He still wasn't thinking of anything as he took aim ...

And was knocked off his feet.

Greco thought he had been shot. He struggled up again, looked around, and sighted foggily on his victim.

Again he was knocked down.

This time he lay on the ground, trying to draw a bead. He never thought of stopping, for Greco was a craftsman.

With the next blow, everything went black. Permanently, because the watchbird's duty was to protect the object of violence—*at whatever cost to the murderer.*

The victim walked to his car. He hadn't noticed anything unusual. Everything had happened in silence.

GELSEN WAS FEELING PRETTY GOOD. THE watchbirds had been operating perfectly. Crimes of violence had been cut in half, and cut again. Dark alleys were no longer mouths of horror. Parks and playgrounds were not places to shun after dusk.

Of course, there were still robberies. Petty thievery flourished, and embezzlement, larceny, forgery and a hundred other crimes.

But that wasn't so important. You could regain lost money—never a lost life.

Gelsen was ready to admit that he had been wrong about the watchbirds. They *were* doing a job that humans had been unable to accomplish.

The first hint of something wrong came that morning.

Macintyre came into his office. He stood silently in front of Gelsen's desk, looking annoyed and a little embarrassed.

"What's the matter, Mac?" Gelsen asked.

"One of the watchbirds went to work on a slaughterhouse man. Knocked him out."

Gelsen thought about it for a moment. Yes, the watchbirds would do that. With their new learning circuits, they had probably defined the killing of animals as murder.

"Tell the packers to mechanize their slaughtering," Gelsen said. "I never liked that business myself."

"All right," Macintyre said. He pursed his lips, then shrugged his shoulders and left.

Gelsen stood beside his desk, thinking. Couldn't the watchbirds differentiate between a murderer and a man engaged in a legitimate profession? No, evidently not. To them, murder was murder. No exceptions. He frowned. That might take a little ironing out in the circuits.

But not too much, he decided hastily. Just make them a little more discriminating.

He sat down again and buried himself in paperwork, trying to avoid the edge of an old fear.

★ ★ ★

THEY STRAPPED THE PRISONER INTO THE chair and fitted the electrode to his leg.

"Oh, oh," he moaned, only half-conscious now of what they were doing.

They fitted the helmet over his shaved head and tightened the last straps. He continued to moan softly.

And then the watchbird swept in. How he had come, no one knew. Prisons are large and strong, with many locked doors, but the watchbird was there—

To stop a murder.

"Get that thing out of here!" the warden shouted, and reached for the switch. The watchbird knocked him down.

"Stop that!" a guard screamed, and grabbed for the switch himself. He was knocked to the floor beside the warden.

"This isn't murder, you idiot!" another guard said. He drew his gun to shoot down the glittering, wheeling metal bird.

Anticipating, the watchbird smashed him back against the wall.

There was silence in the room. After a while, the man in the helmet started to giggle. Then he stopped.

The watchbird stood on guard, fluttering in mid-air—

Making sure no murder was done.

New data flashed along the watchbird network. Unmonitored, independent, the thousands of watchbirds received and acted upon it.

The breaking, mangling or otherwise stopping the functions of a living organism by a living organism. New acts to stop.

"Damn you, git going!" Farmer Ollister shouted, and raised his whip again. The horse balked, and the wagon rattled and shook as he edged sideways.

"You lousy hunk of pigmeal, git going!" the farmer yelled and he raised the whip again.

It never fell. An alert watchbird, sensing violence, had knocked him out of his seat.

A living organism? What is a living organism? The watchbirds extended their definitions as they became aware of more facts. And, of course, this gave them more work.

The deer was just visible at the edge of the woods. The hunter raised his rifle, and took careful aim.

He didn't have time to shoot.

With his free hand, Gelsen mopped perspiration from his face. "All right," he said into the telephone. He listened to the stream of vituperation from the other end, then placed the receiver gently in its cradle.

"What was that one?" Macintyre asked. He was unshaven, tie loose, shirt unbuttoned.

"Another fisherman," Gelsen said. "It seems the watchbirds won't let him fish even though his family is starving. What are we going to do about it, he wants to know."

"How many hundred is that?"

"I don't know. I haven't opened the mail."

"Well, I figured out where the trouble is," Macintyre said gloomily, with the air of a man who knows just how he blew up the Earth—after it was too late.

"Let's hear it."

"Everybody took it for granted that we wanted all murder stopped. We figured the watchbirds would think as we do. We ought to have qualified the conditions."

"I've got an idea," Gelsen said, "that we'd have to know just why and what murder is, before we could qualify the conditions properly. And if we knew that, we wouldn't need the watchbirds."

"Oh, I don't know about that. They just have to be told that some things which look like murder are not murder."

"But why should they stop fisherman?" Gelsen asked.

"Why shouldn't they? Fish and animals are living organisms. We just don't think that killing them is murder."

The telephone rang. Gelsen glared at it and punched the intercom. "I told you no more calls, no matter what."

"This is from Washington," his secretary said. "I thought you'd—»

"Sorry." Gelsen picked up the telephone. "Yes. Certainly is a mess ... Have they? All right, I certainly will." He put down the telephone.

"Short and sweet," he told Macintyre. "We're to shut down temporarily."

"That won't be so easy," Macintyre said. "The watchbirds operate independent of any central control, you know. They come back once a week for a repair checkup. We'll have to turn them off then, one by one."

"Well, let's get to it. Monroe over on the Coast has shut down about a quarter of his birds."

"I think I can dope out a restricting circuit," Macintyre said.

"Fine," Gelsen replied bitterly. "You make me very happy."

THE WATCHBIRDS WERE LEARNING RAP-idly, expanding and adding to their knowledge. Loosely defined abstractions were extended, acted upon and re-extended.

To stop murder ...

Metal and electrons reason well, but not in a human fashion.

A living organism? *Any* living organism!

The watchbirds set themselves the task of protecting all living things.

The fly buzzed around the room, lighting on a table top, pausing a moment, then darting to a window sill.

The old man stalked it, a rolled newspaper in his hand.

Murderer!

The watchbirds swept down and saved the fly in the nick of time.

The old man writhed on the floor a minute and then was silent. He had been given only a mild shock, but it had been enough for his fluttery, cranky heart.

His victim had been saved, though, and this was the important thing. Save the victim and give the aggressor his just desserts.

GELSEN DEMANDED ANGRILY, "WHY aren't they being turned off?"

The assistant control engineer gestured. In a corner of the repair room lay the senior control engineer. He was just regaining consciousness.

"He tried to turn one of them off," the assistant engineer said. Both his hands were knotted together. He was making a visible effort not to shake.

"That's ridiculous. They haven't got any sense of self-preservation."

"Then turn them off yourself. Besides, I don't think any more are going to come."

What could have happened? Gelsen began to piece it together. The watchbirds still hadn't decided on the limits of a living organism. When some of them were turned off in the Monroe plant, the rest must have correlated the data.

So they had been forced to assume that they were living organisms, as well.

No one had ever told them otherwise. Certainly they carried on most of the functions of living organisms.

Then the old fears hit him. Gelsen trembled and hurried out of the repair room. He wanted to find Macintyre in a hurry.

THE NURSE HANDED THE SURGEON THE sponge.

"Scalpel."

She placed it in his hand. He started to make the first incision. And then he was aware of a disturbance.

"Who let that thing in?"

"I don't know," the nurse said, her voice muffled by the mask.

"Get it out of here."

The nurse waved her arms at the bright winged thing, but it fluttered over her head.

The surgeon proceeded with the incision—as long as he was able.

The watchbird drove him away and stood guard.

"Telephone the watchbird company!" the surgeon ordered. "Get them to turn the thing off."

The watchbird was preventing violence to a living organism.

The surgeon stood by helplessly while his patient died.

FLUTTERING HIGH ABOVE THE NETWORK of highways, the watchbird watched and waited. It had been constantly working for weeks now, without rest or repair. Rest and repair were impossible, because the watchbird couldn't allow itself—a living organism—to be murdered. And that was what happened when watchbirds returned to the factory.

There was a built-in order to return, after the lapse of a certain time period. But the watchbird had a stronger order to obey—preservation of life, including its own.

The definitions of murder were almost infinitely extended now, impossible to cope with. But the watchbird didn't consider that. It responded to its stimuli, whenever they came and whatever their source.

There was a new definition of living organism in its memory files. It had come as a result of the watchbird discovery that watchbirds were living organisms. And it had enormous ramifications.

The stimuli came! For the hundredth time that day, the bird wheeled and banked, dropping swiftly down to stop murder.

Jackson yawned and pulled his car to a shoulder of the road. He didn't notice the glittering dot in the sky. There was no reason for him to. Jackson wasn't contemplating murder, by any human definition.

This was a good spot for a nap, he decided. He had been driving for seven straight hours and his eyes were starting to fog. He reached out to turn off the ignition key—

And was knocked back against the side of the car.

"What in hell's wrong with you?" he asked indignantly. "All I want to do is—"

He reached for the key again, and again he was smacked back.

Jackson knew better than to try a third time. He had been listening to the radio and he knew what the watchbirds did to stubborn violators.

"You mechanical jerk," he said to the waiting metal bird. "A car's not alive. I'm not trying to kill it."

But the watchbird only knew that a certain operation resulted in stopping an organism. The car was certainly a functioning organism. Wasn't it of metal, as were the watchbirds? Didn't it run?

MACINTYRE SAID, "WITHOUT REPAIRS they'll run down." He shoved a pile of specification sheets out of his way.

"How soon?" Gelsen asked.

"Six months to a year. Say a year, barring accidents."

"A year," Gelsen said. "In the meantime, everything is stopping dead. Do you know the latest?"

"What?"

"The watchbirds have decided that the Earth is a living organism. They won't allow farmers to break ground for plowing. And, of course, everything else is a living organism—rabbits, beetles, flies, wolves, mosquitoes, lions, crocodiles, crows, and smaller forms of life such as bacteria."

"I know," Macintyre said.

"And you tell me they'll wear out in six months or a year. What happens *now*? What are we going to eat in six months?"

The engineer rubbed his chin. "We'll have to do something quick and fast. Ecological balance is gone to hell."

"Fast isn't the word. Instantaneously would be better." Gelsen lighted his thirty-fifth cigarette for the day. "At least I have the bitter satisfaction of saying, 'I told you so.' Although I'm just as responsible as the rest of the machine-worshipping fools."

Macintyre wasn't listening. He was thinking about watchbirds. "Like the rabbit plague in Australia."

"The death rate is mounting," Gelsen said. "Famine. Floods. Can't cut down trees. Doctors can't—what was that you said about Australia?"

"The rabbits," Macintyre repeated. "Hardly any left in Australia now."

"Why? How was it done?"

"Oh, found some kind of germ that attacked only rabbits. I think it was propagated by mosquitos—»

"Work on that," Gelsen said. "You might have something. I want you to get on the telephone, ask for an emergency hookup with the engineers of the other companies. Hurry it up. Together you may be able to dope out something."

"Right," Macintyre said. He grabbed a handful of blank paper and hurried to the telephone.

"WHAT DID I TELL YOU?" OFFICER CEL- trics said. He grinned at the captain. "Didn't I tell you scientists were nuts?"

"I didn't say you were wrong, did I?" the captain asked.

"No, but you weren't *sure*.»

"Well, I'm sure now. You'd better get going. There's plenty of work for you."

"I know." Celtrics drew his revolver from its holster, checked it and put it back. "Are all the boys back, Captain?"

"All?" the captain laughed humor- lessly. "Homicide has increased by fifty per cent. There's more murder now than there's ever been."

"Sure," Celtrics said. "The watch- birds are too busy guarding cars and slugging spiders." He started toward the door, then turned for a parting shot.

"Take my word, Captain. Machines are *stupid*.»

The captain nodded.

THOUSANDS OF WATCHBIRDS, TRYING TO stop countless millions of murders—a hopeless task. But the watchbirds didn't hope. Without consciousness, they expe- rienced no sense of accomplishment, no fear of failure. Patiently they went about their jobs, obeying each stimulus as it came.

They couldn't be everywhere at the same time, but it wasn't necessary to be. People learned quickly what the watch- birds didn't like and refrained from doing it. It just wasn't safe. With their high speed and superfast senses, the watchbirds got around quickly.

And now they meant business. In their original directives there had been a provision made for killing a murderer, if all other means failed.

Why spare a murderer?

It backfired. The watchbirds extracted the fact that murder and crimes of violence had increased geometrically since they had begun operation. This was true, because their new definitions increased the possibilities of murder. But to the watchbirds, the rise showed that the first methods had failed.

Simple logic. If A doesn't work, try B. The watchbirds shocked to kill.

Slaughterhouses in Chicago stopped and cattle starved to death in their pens, because farmers in the Midwest couldn't cut hay or harvest grain.

No one had told the watchbirds that all life depends on carefully balanced murders.

Starvation didn't concern the watchbirds, since it was an act of omission.

Their interest lay only in acts of commission.

Hunters sat home, glaring at the silver dots in the sky, longing to shoot them down. But for the most part, they didn't try. The watchbirds were quick to sense the murder intent and to punish it.

Fishing boats swung idle at their moorings in San Pedro and Gloucester. Fish were living organisms.

Farmers cursed and spat and died, trying to harvest the crop. Grain was alive and thus worthy of protection. Potatoes were as important to the watchbird as any other living organism. The death of a blade of grass was equal to the assassination of a President—

To the watchbirds.

And, of course, certain machines were living. This followed, since the watchbirds were machines and living.

God help you if you maltreated your radio. Turning it off meant killing it. Obviously—its voice was silenced, the red glow of its tubes faded, it grew cold.

The watchbirds tried to guard their other charges. Wolves were slaughtered, trying to kill rabbits. Rabbits were electrocuted, trying to eat vegetables. Creepers were burned out in the act of strangling trees.

A butterfly was executed, caught in the act of outraging a rose.

This control was spasmodic, because of the fewness of the watchbirds. A billion watchbirds couldn't have carried out the ambitious project set by the thousands.

The effect was of a murderous force, ten thousand bolts of irrational lightning raging around the country, striking a thousand times a day.

Lightning which anticipated your moves and punished your intentions.

"Gentlemen, *please*," the government representative begged. "We must hurry."

The seven manufacturers stopped talking.

"Before we begin this meeting formally," the president of Monroe said, "I want to say something. We do not feel ourselves responsible for this unhappy state of affairs. It was a government project; the government must accept the responsibility, both moral and financial."

Gelsen shrugged his shoulders. It was hard to believe that these men, just a few weeks ago, had been willing to accept the glory of saving the world. Now they wanted to shrug off the responsibility when the salvation went amiss.

"I'm positive that that need not concern us now," the representative assured him. "We must hurry. You engineers have done an excellent job. I am proud of the cooperation you have shown in this emergency. You are hereby empowered to put the outlined plan into action."

"Wait a minute," Gelsen said.

"There is no time."

"The plan's no good."

"Don't you think it will work?"

"Of course it will work. But I'm afraid the cure will be worse than the disease."

The manufacturers looked as though they would have enjoyed throttling Gelsen. He didn't hesitate.

"Haven't we learned yet?" he asked. "Don't you see that you can't cure human problems by mechanization?"

"Mr. Gelsen," the president of Monroe said, "I would enjoy hearing you philosophize, but, unfortunately, people are being killed. Crops are being ruined. There is famine in some sections of the country already. The watchbirds must be stopped at once!"

"Murder must be stopped, too. I remember all of us agreeing upon that. But this is not the way!"

"What would you suggest?" the representative asked.

GELSEN TOOK A DEEP BREATH. WHAT HE was about to say took all the courage he had.

"Let the watchbirds run down by themselves," Gelsen suggested.

There was a near-riot. The government representative broke it up.

"Let's take our lesson," Gelsen urged, "admit that we were wrong trying to cure human problems by mechanical means. Start again. Use machines, yes, but not as judges and teachers and fathers."

"Ridiculous," the representative said coldly. "Mr. Gelsen, you are overwrought. I suggest you control yourself." He cleared his throat. "All of you are ordered by the President to carry out the plan you have submitted." He looked sharply at Gelsen. "Not to do so will be treason."

"I'll cooperate to the best of my ability," Gelsen said.

"Good. Those assembly lines must be rolling within the week."

Gelsen walked out of the room alone. Now he was confused again. Had he been right or was he just another visionary? Certainly, he hadn't explained himself with much clarity.

Did he know what he meant?

Gelsen cursed under his breath. He wondered why he couldn't ever be sure of anything. Weren't there any values he could hold on to?

He hurried to the airport and to his plant.

THE WATCHBIRD WAS OPERATING ERRATICALLY now. Many of its delicate parts were out of line, worn by almost continuous operation. But gallantly it responded when the stimuli came.

A spider was attacking a fly. The watchbird swooped down to the rescue.

Simultaneously, it became aware of something overhead. The watchbird wheeled to meet it.

There was a sharp crackle and a power bolt whizzed by the watchbird's wing. Angrily, it spat a shock wave.

The attacker was heavily insulated. Again it spat at the watchbird. This time, a bolt smashed through a wing, the watchbird darted away, but the attacker went after it in a burst of speed, throwing out more crackling power.

The watchbird fell, but managed to send out its message. Urgent! A new menace to living organisms and this was the deadliest yet!

Other watchbirds around the country integrated the message. Their thinking centers searched for an answer.

"WELL, CHIEF, THEY BAGGED FIFTY today," Macintyre said, coming into Gelsen's office.

"Fine," Gelsen said, not looking at the engineer.

"Not so fine." Macintyre sat down. "Lord, I'm tired! It was seventy-two yesterday."

"I know." On Gelsen's desk were several dozen lawsuits, which he was sending to the government with a prayer.

"They'll pick up again, though," Macintyre said confidently. "The Hawks are especially built to hunt down watchbirds. They're stronger, faster, and they've got better armor. We really rolled them out in a hurry, huh?"

"We sure did."

"The watchbirds are pretty good, too," Macintyre had to admit. "They're learning to take cover. They're trying a lot of stunts. You know, each one that goes down tells the others something."

Gelsen didn't answer.

"But anything the watchbirds can do, the Hawks can do better," Macintyre said cheerfully. "The Hawks have special learning circuits for hunting. They're more flexible than the watchbirds. They learn faster."

Gelsen gloomily stood up, stretched, and walked to the window. The sky was blank. Looking out, he realized that his uncertainties were over. Right or wrong, he had made up his mind.

"Tell me," he said, still watching the sky, "what will the Hawks hunt after they get all the watchbirds?"

"Huh?" Macintyre said. "Why—»

"Just to be on the safe side, you'd better design something to hunt down the Hawks. Just in case, I mean."

"You think—»

"All I know is that the Hawks are self-controlled. So were the watchbirds. Remote control would have been too slow, the argument went on. The idea was to get the watchbirds and get them fast. That meant no restricting circuits."

"We can dope something out," Macintyre said uncertainly.

"You've got an aggressive machine up in the air now. A murder machine. Before that it was an anti-murder machine. Your next gadget will have to be even more self-sufficient, won't it?"

Macintyre didn't answer.

"I don't hold you responsible," Gelsen said. "It's me. It's everyone."

In the air outside was a swift-moving dot.

"That's what comes," said Gelsen, "of giving a machine the job that was our own responsibility."

★ ★ ★

Overhead, a Hawk was zeroing in on a watchbird.

The armored murder machine had learned a lot in a few days. Its sole function was to kill. At present it was impelled toward a certain type of living organism, metallic like itself.

But the Hawk had just discovered that there were other types of living organisms, too—

Which had to be murdered.

THE END

94

"BETTER TO FIGHT FOR SOMETHING
THAN LIVE FOR NOTHING."

"I DON'T MEASURE A MAN'S SUCCESS BY
HOW HIGH HE CLIMBS BUT HOW HIGH HE
BOUNCES WHEN HE HITS BOTTOM"

"NO DUMB BASTARD EVER WON A WAR BY
GOING OUT AND DYING FOR HIS COUNTRY.
HE WON IT BY MAKING SOME OTHER
DUMB BASTARD DIE FOR HIS COUNTRY."

— GEORGE S. PATTON JR.

The General Who Never Knew the War Was Over!
PICTORIAL HIGHLIGHTS OF THE FIGHTING CAREER OF GEORGE S. PATTON WHO, HOWEVER BRAVE, MADE HIS MISTAKES.
George S. Patton
FROM THE BOOK, "PATTON, FIGHTING MAN," BY WILLIAM B. MELLOR, INCLUDING PERSONAL MEMOIRS OF MRS. PATTON, PUBLISHED BY G.P. PUTNAM'S SONS.
ON NOV. 11 TH, 1885, A HUSKY BOY WAS BORN ON A RANCH NEAR SAN GABRIEL, CAL. AT 8 HE DREAMED OF FIGHTING HEROES AND MADE A REMARKABLE PREDICTION.
GEORGIE, YOU GET TO BED!
NURSE! SOME DAY I'LL BE A GENERAL!
THE OFF-SPRING OF FIGHTING ANCESTORS, YOUNG GEORGE S. PATTON JR. STUDIED MILITARY TACTICS AND PLAYED HARD AT SPORTS.
ONLY A MILE TO GO, GEORGE!
STEP ON IT! I WON'T BE LAST!

BY HARD STUDY HE WON APPOINTMENT TO WEST POINT, WHERE HE TOOK THE HAZING LIKE A SOLDIER GRADUATING 46TH IN HIS CLASS HE WON HIGHEST GRADE FOR MILITARY EFFICIENCY.
WIPE THAT SMILE OFF YOUR FACE—AND SCRUB THE FLOOR!
YES, SIR!

ON MAY 26TH, 1910 HE MARRIED 'BEE' AYER THE GLAMOROUS TOAST OF BOSTON SOCIETY
YOU'RE THE GREATEST GIRL IN THE WORLD!
I LOVE YOU GEORGIE!

IN THE 1912 OLYMPICS PATTON COMPETED IN THE PISTOL EVENT—300 METER SWIM—5000 METER CAVALRY RIDE, AND OUT-FENCED ALL BUT 3 OF THE WORLD'S BEST SWORDSMEN!
LOOK! PATTON NEVER BACKS UP! HE ALWAYS ATTACKS!

THE ONLY ONE WHO EVER STOPPED HIM WAS HIS WIFE, WHEN HE BROUGHT HOME TOO MANY SWORDS FOR HER TO PACK.
GEORGE, YOU LISTEN TO ME!
WAIT, BEE! CAN'T YOU TAKE A JOKE?

IN MEXICO, IN 1916, GEN. PERSHING ORDERED LT. PATTON TO 'FIND' GEN. CARDENAS, PANCHO VILLA'S RIGHT HAND MAN. PATTON DID, AND DELIVERED HIM DEAD TO THE GENERAL.
THEY OUTNUMBER US, LIEUTENANT!
AFTER 'EM MEN! THE GENERAL WANTS CARDENAS!

IN WORLD WAR I, PATTON (NOW A CAPTAIN) BECAME AMERICA'S FIRST FIELD TANK COMMANDER AND SMASHED THE GERMANS AT ST. MIHIEL. HE RODE IN THE LEADING TANK!
THEY DIDN'T LIKE THAT ONE, CAPTAIN!
NICE GOING, LIEUT! WE'LL BLOW 'EM TO KINGDOM COME!

LATER, WHEN HIS TANK BOGGED DOWN NEAR CHEPPY WOOD, PATTON WAS KNOCKED OFF THE TOP AND SEVERELY WOUNDED.
LOOK OUT, CAPTAIN!

DRAGGED INTO A SHELL-HOLE BY HIS RUNNER, JOE ANGELO, PATTON, THOUGH BLEEDING PROFUSELY, CONTINUED TO DIRECT OPERATIONS.
HOW ARE YOU FEELING, CAPTAIN?
NEVER MIND ME! GET THOSE ORDERS TO THE PATROLS!

THEN CAME WORLD WAR 2, AND PATTON, IN MANEUVERS ON THE HOT AMERICAN DESERT, LASHES HIS MEN INTO THE TOUGHEST ARMORED UNIT OF THE WAR.
IT MUST BE 110 DEGREES! WE'RE ALL IN!
C'MON, BOYS, WE'VE GOT TO MOVE ON—FARTHER AND FASTER!
THE HEAT'S GOT ME!

HIS FAITH IN MECHANIZED MIGHT WAS SUPREME. HE 'SOLD' HIS SUPERIORS ON USING TANKS FOR THEIR 'SUNDAY PUNCH'.

WE'LL USE 'EM LIKE CAVALRY! SMASH THROUGH THEIR FRONT— AROUND THEIR FLANKS!

AFTER THE AMERICAN SETBACK AT KASSERINE PASS (AFRICA), PATTON PROVED HIS POINT BY SMASHING NAZI GEN ROMMEL'S CRACK ARMY
YIP—EE! THE KRAUTS ARE ON THE RUN!

IN THE INVASION OF SICILY, PATTON, THOUGH SUPREME COMMANDER, FOUGHT BESIDE HIS MEN IN THE STREETS OF GELA. HE WON THE ISLAND IN 38 DAYS!
THEY'RE EVERY-WHERE, GENERAL!
SURE! ALL THE MORE TO SHOOT AT!

PATTON'S HEART BLED WHEN HE VISITED WOUNDED SOLDIERS. OUTRAGED AT ONE HE THOUGHT WAS FAKING, HE SLAPPED HIM, NOT KNOWING THE LAD WAS BATTLE-SHOCKED
GET UP, YOU GOLD-BRICKER! BRAVE MEN ARE SUFFERING!
I-I-I CAN'T GENERAL!

LATER, REALIZING HIS MISTAKE, PATTON COURAGE-OUSLY APOLOGIZED BEFORE HIS ENTIRE DIVISION.
I WAS ON EDGE— I WAS WRONG— I APOLOGIZE!

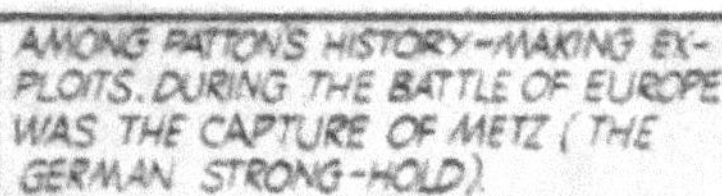

AMONG PATTON'S HISTORY—MAKING EX-PLOITS, DURING THE BATTLE OF EUROPE WAS THE CAPTURE OF METZ (THE GERMAN STRONG-HOLD).
C'MON, BOYS! METZ IS JUST ANOTHER TOWN! LET'S GO!
BUT, AFTER THE WAR PATTON WAS REDUCED TO A 'PAPER' GENERAL, FOR COMPAR-ING NAZIS AND ANTI-NAZIS TO THE POLITICAL STATUS OF DEMOCRATS · AND REPUBLICANS.

FINALLY, ON DEC 21ST, 1945, OLD 'BLOOD AND GUTS' PASSED AWAY IN HEIDELBURG, GERMANY—VICTIM OF AN AUTOMOBILE ACCIDENT. TODAY HE LIES BURIED WITH 6,000 BOYS OF HIS BELOVED 3RD ARMY AT HAMM, LUXEMBURG—WITH 'EM TO THE END!

CONTRIBUTORS

MICHAEL BUNKER is a *USA Today* Bestselling author, off-gridder, husband, and father of four children. He lives with his family in Central Texas where he reads and writes books…and occasionally tilts at windmills. In November of 2015, Variety Magazine announced that Michael had sold a film/tv option for his bestselling novel *Pennsylvania* to Jorgensen Pictures.

ED GOSNEY is a lover of literature and occasionally writes fantastical stories, along with talking about books and comics on his website, edgosney.com. He also helps edit Collectorzine magazine.

ALAN HEWETSON (1946 – 2004) was a Scottish-Canadian writer and editor of American horror-comics magazines, best known for his work with the 1970s publisher Skywald Publications, where he created what he termed the magazines' "Horror-Mood" sensibility.

ROBERT A. KRAUS (RAK) is the creator of Chakan the Forever Man graphic novella series, the Chakan SEGA video game, the Dragon War game system, and many other properties.

HERMAN MELVILLE (1819 – 1891) was an American novelist, short story writer, and poet of the American Renaissance period. Among his best-known works are *Moby-Dick, Typee,* and *Billy Budd, Sailor.* At the time of his death, Melville was no longer well known to the public, but the 1919 centennial of his birth was the starting point of a Melville revival. *Moby-Dick* eventually would be considered one of the great American novels.

EDGAR ALLAN POE (1809 – 1849) was an American writer, poet, author, editor, and literary critic who is best known for his poetry and short stories, particularly his tales of mystery and the macabre.

ROBERT SHECKLEY (1928 – 2005) was an American writer. First published in the science-fiction magazines of the 1950s, his many quick-witted stories and novels were famously unpredictable, absurdist, and broadly comical.

KEVIN G. SUMMERS is the author of *Legendarium, The Man Who Shot John Wilkes Booth,* and *The Bleak December.*

BOOTH TARKINGTON (1869 – 1946) was an American novelist and dramatist best known for his novels The Magnificent Ambersons (1918) and Alice Adams (1921). He is one of only four novelists to win the Pulitzer Prize for Fiction more than once.

THE MAN WHO SHOT

JOHN WILKES BOOTH

★ ★ ★

KEVIN G SUMMERS

AVAILABLE WHEREVER BOOKS ARE SOLD

www.ingramcontent.com/pod-product-compliance
Lightning Source LLC
Chambersburg PA
CBHW080841160726
47999CB00009B/2966